"I'm supposed to be seducing you."

"You've been seducing me all night," he said, leading her into the living room, slipping her purse off her shoulder and deftly tossing it aside.

"That dress, the way you smile, the curve of your neck, the way you plucked at your skirt in the car as we got closer to the house...all seduction."

"I had no idea those little things could be considered seduction," Lizzie said, and her mouth went dry.

Sam sighed. "Neither did I." He sat on the couch and pulled her onto his lap. She did not land gracefully, but lost her balance at the last second and landed pretty hard. He caught her, held her, guided her into a leaning position and began to kiss her throat. One hand slid slowly up her thigh, just barely slipping under her skirt and then stopping. Now, *this* was seduction.

Dear Reader,

You hear it all the time. "Write what you know." Well, I've never been a private investigator, never owned a taser, never had a nutcase come after me. But years ago I did paint my living room a lovely color—Blush—that my entire family (all male, I should point out) insisted was pink. And when I painted a room or two Sahara Sand not so long ago, I heard the same accusation. Pink. (They were mistaken both times. Sorta.) So when Lizzie started painting Sam's office, that's where I called on what I know.

And Edgar's Bakery in Birmingham really does make the best strawberry cupcakes ever.

I truly enjoy a reunion story, a love that lasts. And who doesn't love a man who will do anything for a woman? Anything at all. Love of family is something I identify with very strongly. These are the things I drew on for this story. Paint, cupcakes, family, and love. Always love.

I hope you enjoy Sam and Lizzie's story as much as I enjoyed writing it.

Linda Winstead Jones

COME TO ME

BY
LINDA WINSTEAD JONES

MILLS & BOON

First published in Great Britain 2011
by Mills & Boon, an imprint of Harlequin (UK) Limited,
Eton House, 18-24 Paradise Road, Richmond, Surrey TW9 1SR

© Linda Winstead Jones 2010

ISBN: 978 0 263 88527 9

46-0511

Harlequin (UK) policy is to use papers that are natural, renewable and recyclable products and made from wood grown in sustainable forests. The logging and manufacturing processes conform to the legal environmental regulations of the country of origin.

Printed and bound in Spain
by Blackprint CPI, Barcelona

Linda Winstead Jones is a bestselling author of more than fifty romance books in several subgenres—historical, fairy tale, paranormal and, of course, romantic suspense. She's won a Colorado Romance Writers Award of Excellence twice. She is also a three-time RITA® Award finalist and (writing as Linda Fallon) winner of the 2004 RITA® Award for paranormal romance.

Linda lives in north Alabama with her husband of thirty-seven years. She can be reached via www.eHarlequin.com or her own website, www.lindawinsteadjones.com.

For Kira Sinclair and Kimberly Lang. I'm so honoured and thrilled to be around to see you both succeed, and to celebrate your accomplishments. I know there will be many more.

Chapter 1

"You weren't at the funeral," Lizzie blurted. It was an awkward way to start a conversation with a man she hadn't seen in nearly eight years, but she had a bad habit of saying whatever popped into her head. It was a trait that had gotten her into trouble more than once in her twenty-four years.

Sitting on the other side of a massive, polished walnut desk, Sam's sharply featured face revealed no emotion as he said, "I was out of town and didn't find out about your dad's accident until days after the funeral. I'm so sorry. He was a good man and a good cop. Did you get the card?"

"Yes. Thanks for the thought." The card had arrived nearly four months ago—a week after the funeral—and she'd almost thrown it out in a childish fit. Since Sam had been away, she supposed he could be forgiven for missing the funeral. It wasn't as if she'd gone to any trouble to hunt him down and share the news. She'd been in shock, at the time.

In a completely perverse manner, Lizzie wished this man she'd once had a heart-wrenching teenage crush on had gotten bald or fat or horribly wrinkled in the years they'd been strangers. She wished she could write off her memory of him as the perfect specimen of a man as childish fiction. She wished she could laugh at her stubborn and unwanted habit of comparing every man she met to this one.

Instead, Sam Travers, once her father's partner with the Birmingham police force and currently a successful private investigator, carried the years well. Too well. He was as perfectly handsome as she remembered. His dark hair, cut fairly short but gently mussed, was as thick as ever, and his eyes were even bluer than she remembered. There wasn't an ounce of fat on his now-thirty-two-year-old body, and the only wrinkles she could see were very faint lines around his fantastically blue eyes, lines that only made him more attractive. He wore a perfectly fitted suit these days, instead of the uniform or jeans and T-shirts she remembered, and she was dying to ask him how he'd gotten the small, almost invisible scar on his right cheek—but she didn't.

Lizzie squirmed in her chair, uneasy and questioning her decision to be here. When planning her wardrobe for the day she'd purposely dressed down, determined not to make herself attractive for a man who didn't deserve such efforts. Now she realized she should've gone to someone else. Sam looked a little harder than she remembered. He wouldn't understand. This would never work!

The problem was she didn't trust anyone else. Not with this.

"I have a sister," she said, carefully placing the letters she'd found in her father's papers on Sam's desk and, after a brief pause, pushing them toward him with both hands. "Half sister, that is. I should say *probably* a half sister. If you read the letters, you'll see there's some question about that, though Dad seemed pretty sure. Her name is Jenna. According to these letters she'd be twelve years old now."

Sam glanced at the short stack of envelopes but didn't pick them up. "I'm sure finding out that you might have a half sister was a shock. What exactly do you want me to do?"

"Find her," Lizzie said sharply, perturbed that Sam hadn't figured out that part of it for himself. Some private investigator he was! The word from her father's old cop buddies was that Sam was the best, a fixer of momentous problems, a man for whom no case was too difficult. He took on the toughest court assignments as well as private cases, and had built what had once been a one-man business into a well-respected agency.

"And?" he queried, tapping one long finger on the top letter in an annoying and strangely sensual rhythm.

Lizzie shook her head, annoyed—mostly with herself. "*And* what? Just find her!"

Sam's face remained emotionless, as if he were totally unaffected by her outburst, but there was a hint of something in his eyes that might've been irritation. Sam and her father had been partners for almost three years, the new kid and the veteran striking up a deep friendship in spite of their age and lifestyle differences. There had been plenty of fishing trips and cookouts in those three years, birthday parties and football Saturdays. For those three years, Sam had almost been family. Lizzie remembered him being handsome and funny and one of the good guys. She remembered how he'd casually winked at her on occasion, the same way he probably winked at every other female who crossed his path. She didn't remember him being so steely.

He leaned back in his chair as if relaxing, but the muscles in his body remained tense. He was *not* relaxed. "Odds are this little girl knows nothing about you or the question about her parentage. You might stir up a lot of dust that's best left settled."

She wasn't an idiot; she'd thought of that. "For now, I only want to know where the girl is and that she's okay. I was only eleven or so when Monica was around, but I remember her fairly well." Lizzie instinctively wrinkled her nose. "Monica Yates was one of the unfortunate string of inappropriate girlfriends Dad experimented with after Mom left. From what I recall, she wasn't exactly brilliant mother material, so it only makes sense to check on the girl. If Jenna is happy and well cared for and in a safe place, I won't shatter her world." How dare Sam not even *consider* that a girl who was most likely her father's daughter by another woman might want a big sister!

Stoic and unshakable, Sam stared at her. Sadly, Lizzie's girlish crush on Sam Travers had not entirely dissipated. He was hot, even now. He was the kind of man who could give a girl shivers just by walking past or glancing in her direction. Maybe she should've dressed better and put on some makeup, after all. If he so much as winked at her now she'd probably tremble and tingle in all the wrong places. There might even be drool involved. She might embarrass herself completely with a nervous giggle. Too bad his wife was such a bitch.

"I can afford you, if that's what you're worried about," Lizzie said, digging her checkbook out of her oversize brown leather purse and slapping it on Sam's desk. "I have a successful business, and Dad left me some money, so paying your fee is not a problem."

Now Sam *really* looked annoyed. His lips thinned and his eyes grew cold. "I don't want your money."

"But…"

"I won't take your money," he said sharply, "not under any circumstances."

At least it sounded as if he was considering taking her case. "Well, I won't take charity, not even from you."

He leaned forward and drummed his fingers against the desk. His lips thinned a bit more. Yep, he was definitely irritated. Irritated and macho and apparently accustomed to getting his way in all things.

"How about a trade?" Lizzie dropped her checkbook into the bowels of her purse. "You find Jenna for me, and I paint your office." She glanced with undisguised disdain at the flat off-white walls.

Sam's eyes narrowed. "I don't want a mural of any kind on my walls."

"That's good, because I don't paint murals." Not anymore. Yes, there had been a time when she'd been into landscapes and bowls of fruit, and between the ages of twelve and fourteen she'd painted an insane number of fairies and woodland creatures and kittens. Lots of kittens. She'd painted an awful fairyland mural on her bedroom wall at one point. She shuddered at the memory.

As an adult she'd all too soon recognized that she was a competent but mediocre artist. Maybe she could eke out a living painting Elvis on velvet or kittens with big eyes, but she'd discovered that her real gift was in reviving dull, lifeless rooms. "I paint interiors." She shifted her gaze to stare at the wall behind Sam, and she let her mind go, the way she did when she worked. A calmness settled over her. "These walls would look great in cinnamon taupe. I'd do the trim in heirloom lace, I think. Maybe California cream or Carolina beach beige."

"You paint walls."

"Isn't that what I just said?"

Sam shook his head. "Fine, we have a deal. I'll find this maybe half sister of yours, and you paint my office. But…" He grabbed the letters and drew them toward him as he leaned slightly forward. "If this child's life is settled and she's happy and safe, you steer clear." He used a voice that was cool and demanding. It was the voice of a man who expected his every word to be law. "It wouldn't be nice to drop a bomb like this on a kid."

Lizzie didn't argue that she didn't think of herself as a bomb of any sort. If she argued, Sam might change his mind. "Deal." She stood and offered her hand across the table in a businesslike manner. Sam stood and took it. His hand was warm and large and strong, and she liked the way it felt around hers. To keep from sighing in delight, or perhaps jumping across the desk for a kiss, she asked, "So, how's that bubbleheaded wife of yours?"

Sam dropped Lizzie's hand. "I'm divorced."

"Oh," she said, blushing prettily.

"Six years now." And the marriage hadn't been good for two years before they'd ended it formally.

"That's…" Lizzie stammered, she pursed her lips, her hazel eyes cut to the side and she shook her chestnut hair, most of which was currently caught in a long, thick ponytail. The bangs and wayward strands which had fallen out of the ponytail danced softly. "Heaven help me, I can't say I'm sorry. I can't force the words from my lips." Her voice was quick, as if the words tumbled out of their own volition. "I can't even say 'that's too bad' because it's not. Dottie Ann was no-where near good enough for you. Gorgeous, yes, and heaven knows she had the kind of body you guys make yourselves fools over, but she didn't have half a brain and she was so incredibly selfish. Dottie Ann, what a ridiculous name for a woman who's under eighty. Dad told me she got weird on you after the shooting, which I completely understand. No, no, I don't understand her reaction. I don't get it at all. I understand what happened when you shot that guy, that's what I was trying to say. Dad said you were totally justified. I don't know why he didn't tell me you got divorced. Six years." She took a moment, perhaps lost in a flash of mental math. "I had just moved to Mobile and started school, and I guess Dad thought I didn't need to know."

Sam felt the ice settle in his gut. No one mentioned the shooting. That was in the past. Nothing had ever been out of bounds for Lizzie, though, and apparently that hadn't changed. Her father had been one of the few who'd stood by him in those dark days, even though their official partnership had ended. Sam hadn't seen Lizzie at all during that time. She'd been sixteen; he'd been angry and took to drinking too much, for a while.

It was no surprise Charlie hadn't taken him home during those bad days. He was surprised Charlie had talked about the shooting with his daughter at all. He'd always been determined to protect his little girl. Even from Sam, apparently.

Was that why Charlie hadn't told Lizzie about the divorce? No, it was probably much simpler than that. Two years after the shooting he and his old partner had grown apart. They'd been busy; their lives had taken them in different directions. Later on—just a few years ago— they'd reconnected, but things had never been the same.

"He was *so* mad about that," Lizzie continued. "That she didn't stick beside you like any decent wife would've. That's only one strike against her, in my book. That first time y'all were at the house together, not long before you got married, she told me that maybe one day I would be passably pretty if I lost some weight and outgrew my awkwardness and the rest of my face caught up with my nose and I grew or purchased boobs. Who says that to a fourteen-year-old?"

The conversation was not a happy one; it had stirred up a lot of memories best left buried, and still Sam smiled. "Same old Lizzie, I see. You never did have a problem saying exactly what you think."

She pursed her lips together, as if physically trying to restrain herself.

Amy Elizabeth Porter had grown up to be more than passably pretty. She'd lost a little baby fat, though in spite of Dottie Ann's cruel words she hadn't had a lot to spare. Her face had most definitely caught up with her nose, and the long limbs that had once been awkward were now elegant and sexy—even though she obviously didn't dress to call attention to herself. The jeans she wore were a little bit baggy, and the dark green button-up blouse was at least two sizes too large. Still, Lizzie had a model's bone structure and legs that went on and on. She'd grown into herself very nicely— even if she didn't have what anyone would call a curvaceous figure.

She'd changed dramatically, but for the mouth, which looked fine—more than fine, to be honest—but still opened too often and too freely.

Dottie Ann had been an idiot to say those things to a child. Why hadn't he seen what she was like before it was too late? Ah, yes, thinking with the little head. His wife had always had plenty to say about his partner's young daughter. She'd picked up on the crush Sam had been oblivious to, and for some reason she'd been jealous of a shy, gawky kid. Maybe Dottie Ann had seen what Sam had not; that Lizzie would grow into the beauty before him, that even as a child the barely teenage girl had something Dottie Ann never would. Quality. Character. Heart.

"I'll read the letters and start doing some research." Maybe Lizzie was right to be concerned. After his wife had run away from home like a petulant teenager, leaving her husband and her eight-year-old daughter behind, Charlie hadn't exactly been the best judge of women. His heart had been broken and he'd pretty much given up. Some of his girlfriends in those early single-father years would've given Dottie Ann a run for her money, and Monica Yates had been among the worst.

"When can I start painting?" Lizzie surveyed his office, mentally dissecting the room.

"This weekend," he said. The office would be pretty much deserted, so he wouldn't have to worry about subjecting his employees and clients to paint fumes. By then he'd have all the information Lizzie wanted. He'd hand over the info, she'd slap some paint on the walls, and they could part ways one more time.

She placed a huge and heavy purse on her shoulder, thanked him, and then turned to leave his office. Near the closed door she stopped and turned, pinning calculating eyes on him. Hell, she had Charlie's eyes, and they saw too much. Always had. Did she see too much now?

"You'll call me if you find anything before Saturday?"

"Yes. I have all your information." Address, phone number, cell number.

She nodded. "If I don't hear from you before then, I'll see you Saturday morning. Sevenish?"

"In the morning?"

She laughed, and it was nice. Lizzie had a real, unfettered, no-holds-barred laugh. "Yes, in the morning. Too early for you? You have big plans Friday night?"

"No plans," he said. Though he did like to sleep in on the weekends, if he wasn't working a case.

"Interesting," she said, rocking back on her heels a bit. "Sam Travers with no plans for Friday night. My, my, how the world has changed."

He ignored the bait. "Sevenish it is."

Maybe if he hadn't been so strangely intent on Lizzie, he would've realized sooner that something was wrong. In the outer office a voice was raised. A door slammed.

And then something crashed. Lizzie's head snapped around.

Sam rushed to the door and instinctively placed Lizzie behind him. Raised voices in the front office joined yet another crashing, crackling noise. He reached for the semiautomatic he wore in a leather shoulder holster.

"A gun?" Lizzie sounded surprised. She shouldn't have. Maybe his jacket was cut to hide the fact that he was armed, but she knew what he did for a living. He found people and uncovered secrets. Most people wanted their secrets to remain buried, and now and then they got upset when he dug them up.

"Stay here," he ordered, but it was too late. He heard quick footsteps in the hallway, as well as his receptionist Marilyn's crisp order for the man to stop. Sam looked down at Lizzie, hoping she minded better than she had as a child. "Get under the desk."

"Are you joking?" she asked.

"I don't joke." He gave Lizzie a gentle shove that sent her reeling back, and with a sigh she obeyed his order and turned for the desk.

Sam opened the door, the gun in his hand down and casually concealed behind his thigh. He didn't intend to use it; hadn't actually shot at anyone for years. But there was no threat like a confidently wielded firearm. "What's all the commotion?" he asked calmly, his eyes pinned on the man who was striding toward Sam's office with a baseball bat clutched in one hand.

Jim Skinner, who'd tried to scam an insurance company after "falling" in a chain store in a new upscale shopping center, had not been happy with Sam's photographs and testimony. You'd think a man who was pretending to be laid up with life-altering injuries would know better than to take his girlfriend out dancing, but some guys weren't bright.

"You meddling son of a bitch," Skinner mumbled.

Sam maintained a calm voice. "I was only doing my job, man. Take it easy."

"Take it easy? How can you tell me to take it easy?"

He raised the baseball bat, and Sam made an easy, smooth move that revealed his weapon. At the sight of the sleek semiautomatic, Skinner went still. At least he wasn't stupid enough to think he could take on an armed man with a bat. "Big man with a gun," he said softly. "Not that I'm surprised, you lowlife. I'll bet there are hundreds of people in Birmingham alone that want you dead. You sleep with that thing?"

"Yep."

Frustrated, Skinner raised his bat and took aim at the hallway wall.

"Stop!"

Sam and Skinner both went still at the sound of Lizzie's commanding voice.

He was going to kill her. Hadn't he told her to hide under the desk? She was just like her father. If anything happened to her...

"Who are you?" Skinner asked, obviously annoyed. His eyes flitted from Sam to Lizzie and back again. "Is this your girlfriend?"

"Good heavens, no. I'm the painter," Lizzie said. "If you put a hole in that wall I'm going to have to patch it, and trust me, that's not a fun job. Have you ever tried to patch a big hole in the wall? Little holes are no big deal, a bit of putty and sanding and you're good. But you can never really get a big hole to look right again, no matter what you do."

"He ruined my life," Skinner said, his focus on Lizzie. "If I'd gotten that money, my girl wouldn't have left, and I could've paid all my bills and started over. No one would've been hurt. These big companies have all kinds of money, and I just wanted a little bit. They never would've missed it."

Lizzie snorted. She was so close behind Sam he could feel her body heat; she all but pressed up against him, glancing around his body to speak to the intruder. He made sure she remained behind him, shielded as much as was possible, given the circumstances.

As usual, she spoke her mind. "If your girl left over money, then she didn't love you and you're well rid of her. You look like a healthy, intelligent guy, so I'm sure if you try hard enough you can find a legal way to pay your bills."

Marilyn and Danny crept up behind Skinner. No one else was in the office this afternoon, just one receptionist and one investigator taking care of paperwork. In the distance, sirens sounded. Marilyn had surely called the police as soon as she'd realized there was going to be trouble.

Skinner heard the sirens grow closer, too, and he panicked. Sam could see the fear on his face. "I don't want to go to jail."

"Then you'd better run," Lizzie said.

Marilyn hung back while Danny took a silent step closer to the man with the baseball bat.

"You all saw me, you'll report me and I'll end up in jail. I'm already in enough trouble, thanks to you. I don't need this."

Lizzie gave another snort followed by a soft "Well, duh. You'd better run fast and far."

A panicked Skinner lifted his bat into a threatening position and rushed forward. Sam raised his gun. Danny ran.

And Lizzie slipped her hand around Sam's body and fired a Taser C2. A *purple* Taser C2, Sam couldn't help but note. The small identifying papers flew from the cartridge. The probes found their target—midbody, perfect shot.

Skinner dropped to the ground. He let loose the bat and shook uncontrollably, making noises that spoke volumes about the misery he was in as electric volts worked through his body. He twitched and cursed and drooled. The sirens were now right outside the door.

Lizzie took her finger off the activation button, ending the stream of electrical current that had taken Skinner to the ground. When that was done, Danny took control of the man, moving the bat several feet away and taking the intruder by the wrist—even though at the moment Skinner was no threat to anyone.

Sam looked down at Lizzie, who stared at the gun in his hand. "Overkill," she muttered.

Chapter 2

Lizzie still couldn't get used to calling this house home. Her father had only lived in it for three years before his death four months earlier, so it had never been *home* to her. Sure, she'd eaten plenty of meals here, and she'd slept in the guest room for a few days when she'd moved back from school in Mobile, but still—she hadn't grown up here.

The house was paid for. Her dad had planned for an easy retirement, and house payments were not on the agenda. He'd sold their old home and moved into this split-level, two-bedroom, one-and-a-half-bath house south of Birmingham proper. This was the smallest house in a nice little neighborhood filled with young families as well as a retired couple or two and at least one other single person. She should've sold the house right away, but in a strange way she still felt her dad here, and she wasn't ready to let him go. Not yet. So she'd given up her rented apartment and moved in three months ago.

"Why didn't you ever tell me?" she asked, her eyes on the framed photo of her father, which she'd placed at the center of the kitchen table. She ate her soup and talked to him as if he were there. "Why didn't you find Jenna after that wacko woman told you to leave them alone? Sure, Monica said they had a good life and that it was possible Jenna wasn't your child, but how could you know she was telling the truth? If you hadn't believed there was a very good chance she was your child, you never would've pressed the issue. Maybe she's yours and maybe she's not, but what if Jenna needs us?" If there was even an iota of a chance that this child was a blood relative—pretty much her only blood relative—she couldn't let the matter go. For now, at least, she would think of Jenna as her sister. No more doubts; no more maybes.

Lizzie played with her soup. She'd been young when her mother had left and she wasn't blind to the fact that yes, that traumatic event colored all her relationships. She was always waiting for the people in her life to leave, and like clockwork, they always did. Her sister deserved better; she would not abandon Jenna if there was any chance the girl needed her.

Maybe she had serious abandonment issues, maybe she was starved for family, and yes, maybe she wanted a sister so badly she was willing to look past all the trouble she was stirring up. Sam was right when he said news like this would turn a child's world upside down, but it just didn't seem right not to at least check on the girl.

Lizzie's soup grew cool and still she stirred and took

the occasional small bite. She'd always dreamed of having a sister. Someone she could talk to. Someone she could tell everything. Someone who would laugh with her and play jokes on Dad and help her choose clothes. Lizzie did not have the fashion gene. In the balancing ways of the universe, surely a sister would. In her fantasies this sister wasn't twelve years younger and living God knows where, but if this was all she had, she'd make it work. If Jenna needed her, that is. If showing up wouldn't ruin the girl's well-ordered life.

"How could you not tell me?" she asked angrily, and then she turned her dad's picture facedown on the table. She missed her father, she grieved for him, she loved him dearly. And still, she was furious with him for keeping this secret. If he'd keep one secret this big, how many others were there? What else didn't she know?

Lizzie had just started loading the dishwasher when the doorbell rang. Startled, she almost jumped out of her skin. Callers were not common here, not since the busy days following the funeral. She wiped her hands on a kitchen towel and headed for the front door. How pathetic that a visitor was a shock! She was so wrapped up in her work that she didn't have a very active social life. No boyfriends, only casual girlfriends since most of her pals had gotten married or moved away from the area, no neighbors she was particularly close to.

Finding Sam Travers on her doorstep was a surprise. Normally she might think it a pleasant one, but the way he was glaring at her, *pleasant* was not the first word that came to mind. He clutched the letters she'd given him in one hand.

"What's wrong? I just left you two hours ago." Hope

welled up in her, almost a physical sensation. "Have you already found her?"

Sam stepped closer, and she moved back, and the next thing she knew he was striding into her house as if he lived there. That gray suit must've been made for him, the way it draped perfectly on his lean—but not too lean—body. He was grace and strength, hardness and beauty. How could a man in a conservative suit be so intimidating?

"Nothing is wrong," he said, "you left me *three* hours ago, and no, I don't have anything to report just yet."

"Oh." The hope that had surged through her died as quickly as it had been born. "Why are you here?" Lizzie longed for the comfort and boundaries of the big desk that had separated them at his office for the majority of her visit. Sam looked bigger, more intimidating in her living room than he had in his office, perhaps because she wasn't prepared to face him here and now. Perhaps because she knew his jacket disguised a shoulder holster and a gun. Perhaps because he wasn't exactly the man she remembered.

He turned accusing eyes to her. "I wanted to make sure you were all right after the excitement at the office."

"After I shocked the guy who was coming after you with a baseball bat, you mean."

"Yes," he said crisply.

"I'm fine." She smiled. "You look so surprised. Do you think my father would raise a daughter who wasn't prepared for anything and everything? Do you think he didn't teach me to defend myself?"

"You use the Taser often?" Sam snapped.

"This was my first time. First time to use a Taser on

a real person, that is. Naturally I've practiced on targets and such. Well, *once* I practiced. I can shoot, of course, but I really prefer a nonlethal form of self-defense." As soon as the words were out of her mouth, she regretted them. Her dad hadn't made any secret of the fact that when Sam had taken down the shooter who'd killed a young cop and wounded two others, it had been a life-changing event. There were those—in the department and out—who thought Sam had acted too quickly and with unnecessary finality, that he should've tried to take the guy alive. No one had said anything so outrageous until they'd found out the shooter was barely seventeen, as if the victim would be less dead if the shooter was older. That one night, that one shot, had ended Sam's time on the force. Apparently it had also eventually ended his marriage. "I didn't mean…" she began, but Sam shrugged her off and changed the subject.

"We also need to talk about your situation," he said. He sounded a little tired. "Before I go any further, are you sure…"

"I wouldn't have hired you if I wasn't sure," Lizzie interrupted. "Why are you being so difficult? Isn't this what you do? Don't you find people for a living? Do you always try to talk clients out of hiring you?"

"If Charlie had wanted you to know about this child, he would've told you years ago."

Lizzie shook a stern finger in Sam's direction. "Don't mention his name to me right now. I'm so annoyed with my father, I swear if he was here right now I'd…I'd…"

"Shoot him with your Taser?"

"Maybe," Lizzie snapped. "He certainly deserves a good shock. He *lied* to me. You're not supposed to lie to the people you love. You're not supposed to keep secrets from your *family*. I have a sister, a *sister* I knew nothing about. Jenna is the only blood relative I have, outside my mother, and he kept her from me. Now I'm supposed to forgive him just because he's dead?"

"There is some doubt about whether or not the girl is actually…"

"Until and unless you prove otherwise, I consider Jenna my sister. If there's even the smallest chance that's the case, I have to approach the situation as if there's no doubt at all."

Sam looked decidedly uncomfortable, and he changed the subject. "How is your mother, by the way?"

"How the hell should I know?" Lizzie turned and headed for the kitchen, angry that stinging tears had filled her eyes. "I haven't seen her in two years, haven't spoken to her since I called to tell her Dad had died. We don't have what you would call a healthy mother-daughter relationship." Too much information, too fast. "Can I get you some coffee? Maybe some soup?"

"No, thanks," Sam said, but he followed her into the kitchen.

Sam walked to the kitchen table, where an almost-empty bowl of soup sat. "I interrupted your dinner."

"I was finished," Lizzie said, fiddling with the coffee-pot so she wouldn't have to face him and reveal her tears. He knew she was still fighting her emotions because she didn't tell him what kind of coffee she was making, which mug she would choose and why, what kind of coffee she'd had that morning, and so on and so on.

He reached out and lifted the thin metal picture frame which lay facedown on the table, righting it to reveal the image of his old partner, his old friend. Lizzie must be really upset with Charlie to put his picture down this way. Sam figured now was probably not the time to tell Lizzie that he'd known about Jenna's existence for years.

That wasn't what Lizzie wanted to hear, not just yet. Hell, not ever.

Lizzie was so much like her father. Charlie had said almost exactly the same words, years ago. *If there's the smallest chance the child might be mine, I can't turn my back on her.* Unfortunately for everyone involved, Monica Yates had had other plans.

"I'm making decaf," Lizzie said, her voice noticeably more steady than before. She'd chased away the tears, buried her emotion deep. "Since you're still here and I don't want to be rude and drink in front of you, would you like a cup?"

"Sure," he said absently, righting Charlie's picture. It wasn't fitting for the man to be facedown on his own kitchen table.

For a moment Lizzie watched while the coffeemaker sputtered and spewed, and then she turned to face Sam, dry-eyed and chin held high. While he hadn't been watching, the young girl he remembered had turned into a beautiful woman. The years hadn't entirely erased the quirks and the awkwardness, but those traits had been softened. She'd bloomed. She'd matured. If she wasn't Charlie's little girl and if they'd met under different circumstances… Who was he kidding? Lizzie Porter was seriously off-limits. She was a client, and that was the beginning and the end.

"If you're going to continue to try to change my mind, then walk away now and I'll hire someone else," she said, stubborn as she'd been as a teenager. "I've wasted enough time. I'm not going to waste another minute arguing with you or anyone else."

He couldn't allow her to hire another investigator. Half the P.I.s in town were hacks who were unqualified, dishonest or both. Besides, in the current position he had some control over what she learned, when and how. Sam was torn between what Charlie had obviously wanted and what Lizzie wanted—needed—to know. She was going to find out the truth, sooner or later, and like it or not, the news would come from him. Before he broke the news to her he wanted to know exactly what sort of situation Jenna was in. Charlie's secrets, Lizzie's pain, Jenna's needs. He was going to have to weigh them all. "That won't be necessary."

"When will you get started?"

"First thing tomorrow morning."

"I suppose you'll do a search on the Internet first. I tried, but I have no patience and it was so *slow,* and there was nothing on a Monica Yates that I thought might be the Monica I was looking for, and besides, I assume you have access to files and sites that I can't touch with a ten-foot pole." She gave him a smile that was slightly strained. "I wonder if Jenna lives very far away or if she's still in Alabama. For all I know she's on the other side of the world. It doesn't matter. I want to see her."

"Leave the details to me." Sam didn't think now was the time to tell Lizzie that her newly discovered sister lived not fifteen minutes from this very house.

Lizzie snatched her bowl of soup from the table, dumped the remains of her sad supper into the garbage disposal, rinsed the bowl and stuck it in the dishwasher. She didn't lean on people; it wasn't her way. So why was she tempted to fall into Sam's strong arms and melt into him? Why did she want to make him part of her world?

Old fantasies died hard, apparently.

He remained silent while she finished cleaning up and then poured two cups of coffee. She remembered that Sam took his black, or at least he had years ago. She liked lots of sugar and cream in her coffee. When she placed the two cups at the kitchen table, where Sam sat as if he belonged there, she sighed, sat and said, "You're right."

"Right about what?" He grasped his mug but didn't take a sip of the steaming coffee.

"I don't want to turn Jenna's life upside down. I don't want to hurt her." She saw the all-too-evident relief on his face, a face that had played a part in all her teenage fantasies—until he'd lost his mind and married a massively chested airhead. "That doesn't mean I want you to drop the case."

He didn't look quite so relieved anymore.

"I want to see her. From a distance, if that's all I can get. Maybe we can find a way for me to meet Jenna without telling her who I am, if she's happy and well cared for."

Sam seemed slightly reluctant, still, but he nodded in agreement before lifting the mug to his lips to take a sip of the decaf. Maybe he'd finish his coffee quickly and leave, since he'd failed in his mission to convince her to give up finding her sister. Maybe he wouldn't finish it at all, but would take that one sip and then find a reason to leave. It was easy for people to do, she had learned, finding a reason to leave.

He put his mug on the table, looked her in the eye and asked, "So, how have you been, really?"

This was different than the conversation they'd had in his office. This was her home, her father's home, and there was something intimate about sitting at the kitchen table. "Good," she answered.

A slow grin spread across Sam's face, transforming it, making Lizzie's heart do strange things she hadn't expected after all this time. "Since I've known you, and we're talking a long time, you have never answered any question with a single word. Never. Good? That's it?"

Something inside Lizzie uncoiled as she lost herself in that grin. A moment later she was telling Sam everything, from her stint at school in Mobile to the founding of her own business, to the funeral he'd missed, to clearing out her dad's stuff and finding the stack of old letters from Monica Yates. He listened. His eyes never glazed over. He didn't look at his watch, not even when she lost her train of thought and rambled a bit. The fading light through the kitchen window marked the passage of time; he refilled their coffee cups and brought sugar and cream to the table for her. It was comfortable and natural, as if the years had fallen away.

Only she wasn't fourteen, there was no clinging, empty-headed wife hanging on his arm, and her father wasn't here with them.

When she asked, he told her the latest news on his family—an oft-married mother who lived in Sarasota, Florida with husband number four, a workaholic brother who lived in Atlanta, a married sister with four kids who lived in Arizona. Sam's father had passed away before she'd met him, before he'd joined the Birmingham police force. His family wasn't physically close, but it sounded as if they e-mailed and spoke on the phone fairly often, and there were occasional reunions. She envied him his family.

After she'd basically filled him in on the past six years of her life and he'd skimmed over his, she asked him the question that had been plaguing her since she'd walked into his office and found him annoyingly handsome and appealing. "So, no girlfriend?"

He was surprised by her question, or perhaps by the blunt way in which the question was delivered. His eyes widened slightly, but then he smiled. "Why do you assume I don't have a girlfriend?"

"You're here. You haven't checked your watch once. No annoyed and neglected woman has called on your cell to see where you are at this late hour. There were no personal pictures in your office, except one of you and Dad and some fish."

"You're quite the detective," he said, and then his eyes hardened, the way they sometimes had during this long day. "No, there's no girlfriend. I like my life as it is, and there's no room in it for a permanent relationship. I've been married once and it didn't work out well. I'm not the devoted husband and father type, so it's just as well Dottie Ann and I called it quits before we made the mistake of reproducing. These days I answer to no one, and I like it that way."

"Don't you want to get married and have kids someday?" Didn't everyone want that?

"That's not for me," Sam said easily, so she knew it was the truth. It was kinda sad that he actually liked being alone.

"I knew it," Lizzie said calmly, determined not to turn this into a deep, serious, uncomfortable conversation that would send him running for cover. She opted for childish teasing instead. "The most telling clue of all is the fact that your socks don't exactly match."

Sam pushed away from the table and glanced down at his feet. "They do so match, dammit."

Lizzie smiled. "Gotcha."

Feelings that she didn't need and he didn't want were too close to the surface at the moment. A childish "made you look" would change the tone, and maybe even make her forget, for a minute or two, that although she'd never actually had Sam, she'd never gotten over him, either.

Chapter 3

Sam sat in a nondescript gray sedan, which was parked across the street from an impressive gated mansion. Finding out precisely where Jenna Aldridge lived hadn't been very difficult, since all along he'd had information Lizzie had not—Monica Yates's last name after she'd married her first husband, one elderly and insanely wealthy Harold Aldridge.

He'd had the information last night before he'd gone to Lizzie's house with the intent of changing her mind about finding the girl who might be her half sister—a fool's errand, and he should've realized that before he got in his car to go to her house. Lizzie was doggedly stubborn. She didn't change her mind. At least the child he'd known had not, and from what he'd seen thus far, the woman was just as mulish.

When Monica Yates had gotten pregnant, Charlie

had been determined to do the right thing. Problem was, Monica had no intention of marrying him. She never had. There was another man in her life, Harold Aldridge, and that was the man she intended to marry. She'd even told Charlie that she couldn't be certain he was the baby's father. Could be Harold, she said. Yeah, right. Sam had suspected all along that Monica had just used Charlie like a sperm donor, to do what Harold could not.

She'd begged Charlie not to tell Harold about their affair. She'd begged him to forget she and the baby existed. That hadn't been easy for Charlie to do. He'd always been a man of responsibility, character and honor. It had taken a lot of phone calls and a few letters—letters Charlie had saved—to convince him that biologically his or not, the child was better off without him in her life. But once she had, Charlie had resisted his own emotional pull and only checked in on Jenna every few years.

Monica's plan had worked well. Before Jenna turned four, her "father" died, leaving mother and child incredibly wealthy. A few years later Monica had remarried—another man with money—and not long afterward she'd passed away suddenly. The ambitious woman had a bad heart, and while she'd had the very best doctors, her surgery had not been successful.

Money couldn't buy everything after all. That must've galled Monica to no end.

Jenna Aldridge had been left in the care of her step-father, one Darryl Connelly. They were rolling in money, Jenna was enrolled in the most prestigious private school in Birmingham, they vacationed all over the world. When Charlie had learned about Monica's death, he'd renewed his interest in Jenna, a girl who might or might not be his daughter. Like Lizzie, he wanted to make sure the child was in good hands.

In the end he'd assured himself she was safe and happy, and even though it had hurt more than he'd admitted to anyone, he'd walked away. All Sam had to do was convince Lizzie to do the same.

The front door to the mansion opened, and a young woman walked out. Jenna Aldridge was taller, more mature than she'd been in the last photo Sam had seen of her. Still, she was twelve years old. A child. A long black car crept slowly around the circular driveway, momentarily blocking Sam's view of the girl. The driver, a large man who probably also served as a body-guard, left the driver's seat to open Jenna's door. The two exchanged a few words. Both smiled. So far so good.

The car headed Sam's way. There was a collection of survey equipment and a stack of very official-looking forms in the backseat, in case anyone decided to question Sam's right to be here. He even had a very fine fake ID that would get him past a quick inspection.

But none of that was necessary. The long car trans-porting Jenna Aldridge to school drove past, and neither of the occupants gave Sam more than a passing glance.

Jenna Aldridge had everything any child could ask for, and to pop in and turn the girl's world upside down with news she didn't want or need would be devastat-ing. Still, Lizzie needed to see what Sam had just seen; she needed to see with her own eyes that this child who might be her half sister was in good hands.

He took a quick picture of the house, not for a moment thinking it would be enough to make Lizzie back off.

Sam had pulled away from the curb and made it to the next corner when a white Jaguar convertible passed him. The blonde at the wheel was heavily made up and dressed in a snug-fitting lightweight sweater that matched her car. Jewelry flashed in the sunshine; bracelets, a gold necklace, a huge ring on the hand that rested on the steering wheel. He watched in the rearview mirror as she pulled into the driveway Jenna Aldridge's car had just exited.

Curious, Sam turned around at the corner and slowly made his way back down the street. The Jag pulled up to the front door, and the blonde exited the flashy car with a bounce in her step. Before she could reach the front door it opened, and Darryl Connelly greeted her with a wide smile and open arms she rushed into with eagerness. Feeling as sleazy as he had in the early days when he'd had to take a lot of unsavory divorce cases in order to pay the bills, Sam lifted his camera and snapped a quick photo.

Interesting.

Lizzie arrived at Sam's office bright and early on Saturday morning, a few minutes before the agreed time of 7 a.m. Sam was already there, going over paperwork, looking much too fresh and chipper for the hour. When had Sam Travers become a morning person?

No suit today, she noted. He looked more like the Sam she remembered, in jeans and a plain gray T-shirt. So where was the gun? She was quite sure it was handy. It was sad, that he felt he always had to have that weapon close. When he'd said he slept with the gun under his pillow, had he been exaggerating?

"Good morning," she said as she rushed into his office with her toolbox and gigantic tub of putty and a roll of plastic. She was dressed for the job in an ancient pair of baggy jeans and an old tee that advertised a local bank. Both were paint splattered, revealing an array of colors she'd used in the past year. She was a walking advertisement for her own work.

Sam glanced up, took in her attire and smiled. "Did you manage to get any paint on the walls?"

"Very funny." She carefully placed her things on the floor and surveyed the office, trying to decide where to start. The walls really were awful, with dings and dents and holes where pictures had once hung. Sam's office wasn't only dull, it was imperfect. It was seriously flawed. This she could fix.

"What are you doing?" Sam asked when Lizzie began to move the chairs on the east side of the room away from the wall.

"I'm paying for your investigative services," she said, not bothering to look his way.

"You're not moving furniture," he insisted, and she could hear his chair scrape back as he stood.

"I am," she said.

"You are not," he replied.

Lizzie turned to stare at the stubborn man for a long moment. "Do you expect me to paint *around* the furniture?"

"I'll move the furniture," he said, almost, but not quite, clenching his teeth.

"It's part of the job, part of my payment for your services. Geez, Sam, I work alone more often than not, and I've moved my fair share of furniture. It's not like you have an armoire or a sleeper sofa. This I can handle."

He stepped away from the desk. "Let me…"

"Am I going to have to ban you from your own office for the duration?"

He stopped short. "What duration? You'll finish today, right?"

Lizzie grinned. "No way. I don't just slap paint on a wall and call it done. This is at least a three-day job. Maybe four."

"You're kidding."

"Five days minimum if you don't let me get to work."

He didn't like the idea, but he did finally return to his desk, sit and grudgingly allow her to do what she'd come here to do. The east side of the room didn't have a window, which made it a good place to start. She moved the furniture away from the wall—nothing heavy, just a small table with an artificial plant sitting on it and an uncomfortable-looking chair—and laid out her drop cloth. The putty she used wasn't horribly messy, but sometimes she got carried away. Better safe than sorry. She tried to ignore the fact that Sam was in the room, but it wasn't easy. She was going to have to tell him that he didn't have to stay here and watch her the whole time. She liked to work alone. Usually she set up her portable CD player and popped in some music and got lost in her work. With Sam around, she couldn't get lost in anything!

She took down the framed photograph of Sam and her dad after a long-ago fishing trip, as well as a generic landscape. When she started to remove the nails with the grooved end of her favorite hammer, he stopped her with a chilling question.

"What are you doing?"

Hammer in hand, she turned to face him. "I'm working. Don't you have somewhere else to be?"

"You don't paint with a hammer and I have nowhere else to be but right here."

She curled her lip, slightly. "Must I explain myself step by step?"

"Apparently so." He crossed his arms over his chest, and there was something about the stance he took that made Lizzie's heart skip a beat. When it came to men, she wasn't exactly a novice. She'd dated guys in the past, one or two fairly seriously. She knew quite a few boys, some as friends, some as more than friends— though she'd been without a more-than-friend for a while now. She'd had a few boyfriends, some serious and some not so. Sam was no *guy* and he was no *boy*. He was one hundred percent man, and he affected her differently than any other man or boy or guy she'd ever known. He made her stomach turn over and her mouth go dry. He made her tremble deep down and crave things she should not, could not crave. Suddenly she felt a little defensive, as if she needed to build a wall between her and Sam just to protect her sanity.

"If you don't understand the importance of prep work then I'm not surprised that you don't have a girl-friend." The minute the words were out of her mouth, Lizzie felt a rush of heat in her cheeks. When was she going to learn to think before she spoke? That wasn't exactly the kind of wall she had in mind.

"What the hell is that supposed to mean?"

She tried to pretend she wasn't embarrassed. Since she'd started the conversation, she might as well finish it. "Prep work, laying the foundation, building perfection, taking one's time to make sure that a task is properly done. Detail, Sam, *detail*."

"What does that have to do with me not having a girlfriend?" Frustration was clear on Sam's face, and Lizzie wished once more that she'd kept her mouth shut. Keeping her mouth shut had never been easy for her.

"If you can't figure it out for yourself I'm not going to tell you," Lizzie said as she turned to face the wall before her. She slowly ran a hand across the surface, feeling every bump, every imperfection. Whoever had painted this wall last had simply slapped paint on over a dusty wall. "What trained monkey painted this office?"

Sam remained quiet, and Lizzie was forced to turn to look at him. He was all but steaming. "When we moved into this office building I painted the wall myself."

"Oh," Lizzie said, as she turned to resume her inspection. Yes, no wonder there was no girlfriend. A man who gave so little attention to detail would make a terrible lover. She glanced over her shoulder. Of course, there was nothing that said Sam couldn't learn a thing or two about detail....

Prep work. No girlfriend. Trained monkey.

It didn't take Sam long to figure out what Lizzie meant. Fortunately by the time it hit him she was facing the wall again, displaying an oddly sexy form in loose-fitting jeans and a T-shirt with paint splattered all over it. How exactly had she gotten paint on her back, anyway?

He'd show her prep work, dammit.

Sam had taken two steps from his desk before the force of his foolishness hit him. Lizzie was no longer a teenager with a crush, and the difference between twenty-four and thirty-two wasn't impossible the way fourteen and twenty-two had been. But she was a client, and more important, she was Charlie's little girl.

Charlie had wanted so much for his daughter. She'd deserved better than a mother who left without warning and a father who worked all the time. Maybe if Charlie had found a decent woman and married her, their lives would've been different. It wasn't that he hadn't met and dated any nice women, they just hadn't lasted long. Burned badly by his wife's desertion, Charlie had been unable to trust that what he saw in a good woman was real. The ones who were less than nice—at least they were honest. That had become his skewed way of looking at things.

Lizzie certainly deserved better than a private investigator who could never offer her a permanent relationship. Sam had given up on permanent the day his wife had walked out of his house and directly into another man's arms. He'd given up on permanent when the citizens of the town he'd risked his life to protect had come out to picket the precinct after the shooting. He'd thought his marriage would last forever, that he would be a cop until retirement came along. But nothing was forever, he knew that now.

And kids? Forget it. Working child custody cases only made him glad that he wasn't a father. He couldn't imagine raising a child in this world.

Lizzie was young. She still believed in forever, and he hadn't missed the spark in her eyes as she'd asked about him about wanting a wife and kids of his own. She idealized family and happily ever after; her heart was still whole—and he wouldn't be the one to take that from her.

Though he would like to prove to her that he wasn't entirely clueless when it came to handling women.

Sam grabbed his cell phone and made a quick and almost incoherent excuse before he left his office. He dialed Darryl Connelly's number, wondering how best to approach the situation and absolutely certain that he needed to get this over with ASAP.

A young girl answered the phone with a breathless "Hello."

Sam was momentarily speechless. He'd expected Connelly himself to answer. Maybe a butler or a maid.

In a crisp, businesslike voice, he asked, "May I speak to Mr. Connelly, please?"

"Sure." Jenna barely moved her mouth away from the receiver to shout, "Dar— Dad? It's for you." Sam instinctively moved the phone away from his ear.

His ear was still ringing when Jenna turned her attention back to the caller. "He'll be right here. I hope you don't keep him too long. I have a soccer game and I'm supposed to be there in fifteen minutes. None of the other girls are driven to the games by drivers. Their parents take them. It's *so* embarrassing to be delivered to the school field and dropped off when everyone else shows up with their families. Darryl, I mean Dad, well, he's actually my stepfather but he likes me to call him Dad, he *promised* he would take me to today's game, so whatever you do don't keep him on the phone too long."

Sam took a deep breath. If there had ever been any doubt that Jenna was Lizzie's sister, it had just flown out the window. He quickly dismissed that thought. Many young girls rambled, related to Lizzie or not. "I can see that I called at a bad time. Please tell Mr. Connelly I'll call him on Monday to discuss his insurance needs."

"Yeah, whatever," Jenna said. "I gotta run. Wish me

luck!" With that, the call ended. Sam leaned against the wall and closed his eyes. This was what Lizzie needed, what she'd hired him to do. It wasn't his business if Lizzie got her heart broken. She'd hired him to find the kid, not guarantee a happy ending. He didn't see many happy endings in his line of work.

He stood there for a few minutes, wishing he could make this case go away, wishing he didn't have to deal with a grown-up Lizzie Porter. Best to get this over with. Before he had time to talk himself out of it, he stalked back into the office, walked straight to Lizzie, grabbed her arm and said, "You want to see this girl you think might be your sister? Let's go."

Chapter 4

"I can't meet her like this!" Lizzie said as Sam ushered her out of the building and locked the door behind him.

"You're not going to meet her. You're going to see her from a distance. There's a soccer game at her school and she's playing."

"How do you know that?" Lizzie asked as Sam took her arm and led her toward the parking lot and his boxy gray car.

"I'm a private investigator. It's my job."

He sounded so curt! He was probably still annoyed about the "no details" discussion they'd just had. Men could be so sensitive, especially when it came to their lovemaking skills or their manliness. Sam Travers was a star when it came to manliness. She couldn't even begin to guess about the other, and it would be best if her mind did *not* go there.

Sam was silent as he drove, and for once Lizzie was silent, as well. What did Jenna look like? Were there sisterly similarities or was she her own person, distinct and individual? Maybe Jenna wouldn't even like Lizzie. Maybe she'd think a fully grown sister was lame and unnecessary. Maybe they had nothing in common; maybe they weren't sisters at all.

Jenna had a family—maybe even other siblings by now; she didn't need a sister popping up out of nowhere. Lizzie's physical reaction to the idea of confronting the girl was much like the one she had when she looked at Sam too closely. Jitters. Squirming. Shaking. Only this wasn't quite so…pleasant. She was terrified that her plans were about to go very wrong.

"Turn the car around," Lizzie said abruptly.

"We're almost there."

"This is a mistake." Boy, was it a mistake. Going to Sam's office, digging into old secrets, thinking she could manufacture a family out of thin air…all mistakes, one after another.

"Are you still worried about the way you're dressed?" Sam asked. "Jenna won't see you, I promise. We'll stay back and watch, that'll be it for this time."

Lizzie shook her head. "No, the whole thing is a mistake. Dad was right to keep Jenna's existence a secret. If I meet her I'll blow it, somehow. I always do. I'll open my mouth and say something stupid and that'll be it. Jenna doesn't need me. She already has a family."

Sam didn't argue, but he didn't turn around, either. He turned into the parking lot of a very nice private school, one Lizzie knew to be very expensive. Talk about exclusive! The lot was pretty full, so they had to park at the far end. He pulled into a space away from the other cars, turned off the engine and faced her, one casual hand on the steering wheel, his eyes not at all casual.

"You know that I believe revealing your possible relationship to the girl would be traumatic for her."

Lizzie nodded, the move jerky and too fast. "You were right all along," she said quickly. *So let's get out of here already!*

Sam's face remained even and calm. Did he never show emotion? Did nothing ruffle his feathers? "I also believe you need to see her, even if from a distance. If you don't, you'll regret it later."

She didn't immediately agree or disagree. Maybe he was right. Maybe it was best to get it over with, to get a look at the girl and move on with her life. She was curious, after all. A little curiosity wasn't necessarily a bad thing. "A quick look, then."

"Just a look."

Staring into Sam's calm blue eyes made Lizzie feel calmer herself. Everything would be okay. She'd just have a look to prove to herself that Jenna was well cared for and happy. She flung open the passenger door and stepped out of the car before she could change her mind.

Lizzie was drawn to the sounds of shouting and cheering and the occasional whistle. Sam fell into step beside her, too close, not close enough. She wanted to reach out and take his hand and clutch it, but she didn't. He'd think she was a total wuss if she clung to him just because she was about to get a long-distance look at the girl who might be her sister.

The soccer field was well-groomed, and the girls that played upon it were dressed in blue-and-gold or red-and-white uniforms. The metal bleachers held a collection of parents. Most of them watched the game with genuine interest and excitement. A contingent of younger siblings played in the grass beside the bleachers. It was a scene right out of a Norman Rockwell painting, a healthy slice of family life. If Jenna had a perfect existence, who was she to mess it up?

Not far from the edge of the parking lot, in the shade of an ancient elm tree, Lizzie stopped. "Which one is she?"

Sam studied the players for a moment, and then he pointed. "There, in blue and gold. Brown ponytail. Number 8."

Lizzie's eyes were glued to number 8 when the girl took control of the ball and turned. It was difficult to tell from a distance, but did she look a little bit like their dad? Lizzie's heart thumped. Did she have Charlie Porter's longish nose and narrow eyes? Jenna had that coltish look girls of her age sometimes had, leggy and thin and awkward, on the edge of turning into a young woman, but yes, there was a definite resemblance.

Jenna's brown hair didn't have quite the same slightly reddish tint Lizzie's had, but there wasn't but a shade or two of difference. Not that there weren't thousands upon thousands of girls and women with the same color hair.

Lizzie didn't realize she'd reached for Sam's hand and grabbed on until he squeezed. She knew she should end the contact, let go and maybe take a step away from the man at her side. But she didn't.

"Jenna's mother passed away four years ago," Sam said. "She lives with her stepfather, Darryl Connelly, in what can only be called a mansion. She attends this school, plays soccer and takes ballet, and her yearly allowance is probably about the same as my annual salary."

"Monica died?" Lizzie had never thought Monica Yates would make a decent mother, but for Jenna to lose her mom so young had to be traumatic. Her stomach knotted. At the age of eight they'd each lost their mother—in very different ways.

"Heart troubles, difficult surgery." The explanation was simple, but it was enough.

"Which one is Connelly?" she asked, her eyes turning to the parents.

Sam motioned, this time to the bleachers. "Top row, to the right."

Unfortunately Connelly was one of the parents who weren't watching the game. He gave the attractive woman at his side much more of his attention. Lizzie was incensed, for Jenna's sake. When she'd played softball, her dad had been the loudest, most belligerent parent in attendance. He'd embarrassed her countless times, which was as it should be. This guy didn't even care about the game.

Jenna scored and her team celebrated. Someone sitting near Connelly had to punch him on the arm and tell him that his daughter had scored a goal. He smiled and clapped dutifully, and so did the woman at his side.

Too late.

So Jenna had money. Money was nice; Lizzie wished she had more of it herself, but cash alone wouldn't make anyone happy. She and Charlie had never had much money when she'd been growing up, but they'd gotten by just fine and they'd been happy. Most of the time.

Jenna's teammates congratulated her, and soon the girls lined up at the center of the field to resume play.

"Seen enough?" Sam asked softly.

"No. Yes. I don't know."

He squeezed her hand again and then dropped it, taking a step away from her—as she'd known she should but had not. Lizzie tore her eyes away from Jenna and stared up at Sam. She was suddenly much more certain about what she had to do. "It's not enough. I can't seriously doubt that she and I are related. She looks so much like Dad, and maybe even a little bit like me. Jenna is my family, like it or not. How am I supposed to tell from a distance if she's happy?"

"That fact that she bears a subtle resemblance to Charlie is hardly proof," Sam said sensibly.

Lizzie was in no mood for common sense! "It's proof enough for me." At least for now. "How am I supposed to know that she's *happy*?"

"Trust me, she's…"

Frustrated, Lizzie interrupted. "She has a big house, she goes to a great school, she can buy herself anything she wants. That doesn't mean anything!"

Sam's eyes narrowed. "You said you didn't want to shake up her life."

"Maybe I've changed my mind."

"If your father had thought for a moment that Jenna wasn't safe and content, he would've done something about it years ago," Sam argued.

"Dad let her go as a baby," Lizzie said reasonably. "He couldn't have known whether or not she was okay now."

"Dammit, he did," Sam said sharply. "You're not going to like it but here's the truth. After Jenna's mother died, Charlie kept very close tabs on the kid. If he didn't think it was right to stir up her neat little world, what makes you think you should do it?"

Lizzie no longer stared at her sister. Instead she

glared up into Sam's traitorous blue eyes, and her heart broke as certainly as it had at fourteen, when he'd married an unkind, unworthy woman, whose only claim to fame had been her freakishly large boobs.

The only way Sam could've known that her father had kept tabs on Jenna was if he'd known about the child himself. He'd known all along.

Lizzie was pissed, perhaps rightly so. He should've told her up front that he knew of the girl's existence. Instead he'd tried to spare her feelings; he'd tried to make things easier for her and still honor Charlie's wishes. But at some point he'd decided he didn't want to lie to her anymore, not even by omission.

Ten minutes after leaving the school grounds, after enduring ten minutes of absolute silence, Sam pulled into a bakery parking lot. Lizzie's normally warm hazel eyes shot daggers at him. "You want a doughnut, hotshot, you wait until after you've taken me back to my car."

"No," he said, opening his door and stepping into the spring sunshine. Lizzie remained in her seat, arms crossed over her chest, eyes straight ahead. Sam walked around the car and opened her door as if they were on a date and he was being a perfect gentleman. When she didn't move, he offered her his hand.

"You're fired," she said, ignoring his steady hand. "In case you haven't already figured that out for yourself, Mister Big Shot Private Investigator."

"We need to talk."

"No, we don't."

Sam stood there, hand extended. Lizzie continued to ignore him. "Your purse is back at my office." Lucky for him, considering that there was a Taser in that purse and at the moment Lizzie looked as though she'd gladly use any handy weapon on him. "You don't have your cell phone, cash, credit cards or the keys to your car, which means that until we get back to the office you're at my mercy."

"Cruel *and* a liar."

"I'll buy you a cupcake. That's hardly cruel."

"I don't want a cupcake."

"You always want a cupcake. I also plan to explain myself, if you'll let me." Hell, he was all but begging. Others in the parking lot were starting to stare. If Lizzie didn't hurry up and take his hand, he was going to drag her inside and force-feed her that damn cupcake.

Yeah, that would go over well.

She used one hand to shoo him back, and then she stepped out of the car, moving regally in spite of her baggy, paint-splattered attire, her displeasure evident in every move, every glance. How was it that all women knew how to do that? Was it in their DNA or was there a secret class the men of the world were not privy to? *How to make a man feel two inches tall with a single glance 101.*

They walked into the small bakery and were assaulted by the scents of baking bread and sweets and coffee. A handful of customers were waiting at the counter. Along one window sat a half-dozen small, round tables, each with two hard chairs. All but one was empty, since most of the customers were getting their orders to go. Sam motioned to the nearest table, and Lizzie turned in that direction. She walked past the table he'd indicated and continued on, taking the table farthest away, as if she couldn't stand to be any closer to him.

It was going to be a long conversation.

Eventually Sam reached the counter, where he ordered two coffees, a strawberry cupcake, four chocolate chip cookies, a piece of peanut butter fudge and a blueberry muffin. Ten years ago strawberry cupcakes had been Lizzie's weakness. He couldn't be sure what she preferred now, and he wanted to be prepared.

When he had his order in hand, Sam turned away from the counter, not a hundred percent certain he'd find Lizzie where he'd left her. She was mad—rightfully so, he supposed. Knowing her, she might hitchhike to his office and break into the building to retrieve her purse. She could borrow a cell from a stranger and call a friend to collect her. She could walk home. The walk would take her half a day, but that didn't mean she wouldn't try. He didn't for one minute think she was helpless. If she stayed, it was because she wanted to hear what he had to say.

His eyes fell on the empty table where Lizzie had once sat, and he groaned. He'd hoped she might be willing to listen. He'd hoped she'd have an open mind. Yeah, he'd hoped she'd be where he'd freakin' left her. His eyes flitted to the parking lot, but if she was gone then she'd left minutes ago, while he'd been dealing with the girl behind the counter. She wouldn't stick around and give him the chance to catch up with her and try to change her mind.

As Sam's heart sank into his stomach, Lizzie brushed by without sparing a glance for him or his purchases. She held a stack of napkins, stirrers, sugar and little containers of creamer in her hands. She returned to the table where he'd left her, slapping the napkins onto the center of the table and then sitting, lifting her head to glare at him once more. *How to tell a man he's scum without ever saying a word.*

He smiled.

She didn't like it.

Sam placed the coffee and goodies—which were all stored in a large white bag—on the center of the round table. Lizzie took one of the coffees and removed the lid, fixing it as she liked, with lots of sugar and creamer. She didn't look at him while she stirred, not until he sat, reached into the bag and drew out the cupcake, which was large and pink. The thick frosting was dotted with tiny bits of real strawberries.

It wasn't his imagination that her expression softened a little. "You remembered."

"How could I forget? While we were working together, your dad brought me here every year on your birthday so he could buy your favorite strawberry cupcakes."

She took the sweet from him and began to gently pull away the paper cup to expose the cake. "Fine. The cupcake has bought you a brief reprieve. You can explain now." She glanced up at him, eyes narrowed. "It had better be good."

Lizzie picked at the cupcake while Sam talked. It had been foolish of her to make Sam Travers any more than he was, in her apparently irrational mind. He was no knight in shining armor, no noble and perfect man whose honor would never allow him to tell a lie. He was just a man like any other, skating through life the easiest way he knew how, lying when it was convenient, doing whatever was necessary to get his way.

He told a good enough story, she supposed. Whatever he'd done, he'd done for her father, who really had been a good man. Noble and all that. Charlie hadn't wanted his little girl to know that he'd screwed up so royally; he hadn't wanted her to know she had a sister she could never meet. Her father had been trying to spare her the pain he experienced in having a child he couldn't claim; Sam had been trying to spare her the pain of realizing how completely her father had lied to her. So, who was going to spare her the pain of dealing with overly protective men? No one, apparently.

Charlie had been certain, it seemed, that Jenna would be better off without them. She had a decent stepfather; all that money; a nice, stable, privileged life. Sam had kept that secret until now because Charlie had asked him to keep the secret.

Sam even suggested that Charlie had been afraid that if he pushed the matter there would be a paternity test, and what if it turned out he wasn't Jenna's father after all? He'd come to love the child from a distance, and to be dragged into court and have the belief that the girl was his daughter ripped away would've been more than he could bear. Too, he was thinking of Jenna. They wouldn't have been able to keep the suit a secret, and she'd know what kind of woman her mother was.

Some men would've been relieved to be let off the parental hook. Some men would've forgotten the child at the first opportunity. Not Charlie. He wasn't built that way.

Lizzie so wanted to stay angry with Sam, and if she tried very hard she could. For a while. Why was she still such a sucker for Sam Travers and his blue eyes? Why did she fold so easily? As she picked at the cupcake and sipped at her coffee, her anger melted—but she wasn't yet ready to let Sam see that she was on the verge of forgiving him. Staring at the cupcake instead of him and remaining unnaturally silent should let him know that she was still displeased. The fact that she didn't get up and storm out or punch him in the jaw should also tell him that she was not beyond all reason.

Sam was her father's friend, even now. A friend kept secrets. A friend remained protective even after death.

That didn't mean he should get off too lightly.

After he'd explained why he hadn't told her everything the day she'd hired him, Sam sighed and took a sip of his own cooling coffee. There were lots of goodies in the bag on the table, but he didn't touch any of them.

"Let's talk about Jenna," he said, his voice lowered so no one nearby would hear.

"She's my sister, and I don't think I like her stepfather."

Sam raised his eyebrows. "She might be your sister, and you only saw Connelly from a distance. How can you tell that you don't like him?"

"Jenna looks too much like Dad to believe for a minute that she's not his." Maybe she was like her father and simply wanted to believe it was true. "Connelly wasn't watching the game. He was too interested in the skank who was sitting with him."

Sam reached into the bag and came out with a chocolate chip cookie. "*Skank* is a little harsh, don't you think? Connelly's wife's been gone four years. He's allowed to date."

"Jenna should be his top priority, at least until she's grown. Do you really think a woman like that one is a good influence on a young girl?" Lizzie ignored the fact that her own dad had been dating Monica when she was the same age.

"For all you know she's sweet and nurturing."

"Ha! Women who look like that one don't want to be bothered with taking care of kids."

"You can't judge a book by its cover."

Lizzie sighed. "Now you're resorting to clichés. I'm so disappointed."

"I suppose you want me to investigate her, too," Sam said, only slightly sour.

"Of course! Did you doubt it for a minute?"

"Nope."

"I want to get into the house," Lizzie said. "I won't be satisfied until I see Jenna close-up, talk to her and check out where she lives."

"Maybe we can find a way to do a discreet DNA test."

"I'm sure of the results, but if it makes you feel better, why not?"

"Sibling DNA comparisons aren't as simple as a paternity test, and the fact that you're half siblings makes it more difficult. On Monday I'll call a company I've used in the past and ask them how we should proceed."

She finally looked Sam directly in the eye. "You do that, if it makes you feel better, but I'm not waiting weeks for DNA results. If you're really sorry you lied to me, if you truly want to make amends, then get me into that house."

"It won't be easy," he said.

Lizzie lifted a glob of strawberry icing with the tip of her little finger and raised the pink frothy frosting toward her mouth. "If it was easy, I'd do it myself."

Chapter 5

Getting the silent treatment from Lizzie was torture. Fortunately for Sam, she wasn't particularly good at keeping her mouth shut, and her version of the silent treatment only lasted a day and a half. He should've been grateful for the silence during that time, but strangely he was not.

Lizzie Porter was everything he didn't want in a woman. She was too young, too optimistic, too bright-eyed. She talked too much and very often said whatever was on her mind, as if her every thought came spilling out unchecked. Her clothes were not at all sexy. In fact, just the opposite. It was as if she went out of her way not to call attention to herself. Those clothes, as well as at least a small portion of her flawless skin, were more often than not splattered with paint or putty. She usually had some kind of gunk under her fingernails.

But man, she had a lush mouth that would stop traffic, and her eyes were smart, and her body was tight and tempting. Watching her prep his office for paint was torture. If she wasn't Charlie's daughter, he'd…

No, he wouldn't. Sam turned his eyes back to the papers on his desk, not reading them but doing his best to look as if he were engrossed. Not that Lizzie paid him much mind as she patched and sanded.

She'd spent the large part of two days—the entire weekend—prepping the walls, and today she'd paint. He couldn't wait for her to finish the job and get out of his office so he could concentrate again. She was a constant distraction. It didn't help matters at all that she'd taken to wearing a small MP3 player. It was probably her way of tuning him out, even though she had deigned to speak to him again. The music she was listening to must be quite rhythmic, judging by the way she very slightly moved her hips as she hummed along.

Since she couldn't carry a tune, he didn't have a prayer of deciphering exactly what she was listening to, but the sway of her hips was torture. It wasn't exactly a bump and grind, but the rhythm was there and it made his mouth water. Just what he didn't need.

Most everything in the office but him was covered in plastic as Lizzie removed the lid from a five-gallon bucket of paint and dipped her brush inside. Moving very carefully, she began to cut in along one window with a steady hand. No painter's tape for Lizzie. Her hand was steady and the line was perfection.

Sam watched the paint go onto the wall as he stood slowly. "Lizzie, it's pink!"

She heard his voice through the earbuds and turned her head, removing one of the tiny buds. "What?"

Sam pointed. "Pink. You're painting my walls *pink!*"

She sighed. "This is not pink, it's cinnamon taupe. You just can't see the color properly because you're a man and your inadequate eyes cannot properly discern pigments." She wagged the brush at him, splattering her shirt with paint. "If you were gay you'd be able to see the color as it was meant to be seen."

"What?"

"Never mind," she said. "Trust me. This is the perfect color for these walls. It's warm and gentle and will put your clients at ease. Maybe you'll even stop being so grumpy when you're surrounded by a proper color. These walls don't want to be boring off-white or angry green or sallow yellow, they want to be gentle, soothing cinnamon taupe."

"It's pink," he said again.

"No, it's not." Lizzie completely ignored him and returned to her painting. He could insist that she stop and choose another color, but judging by their conversation thus far it would be easier to let her do what she wanted and then repaint the walls himself after she was done. Trained monkey that he was.

When the phone rang Sam was glad of the interruption. Insurance scams, missing spouses or runaway teens, hell, even a cheating husband would be a welcome change of pace. Anything to take his mind away from pink walls and tempting painters.

Unfortunately the call didn't take his mind off Lizzie at all. The idea he'd put into motion early that morning had already paid off. It was amazing what a substantial bribe to an underpaid and unappreciated employee could do.

He hung up the phone and turned to face Lizzie, who continued to shake her fine ass as she painted his walls a dull shade of pink. No matter what she said, that *was* pink, dammit. Instead of shouting over the music in her ears he walked up behind her, removed one of the buds, and when she spun around to face him, he told her the news.

"Starting on Thursday, you'll be working in Connelly's house. You'll paint Jenna's bedroom, as well as..."

He didn't get any further. Lizzie laughed and threw herself at him, squealing, wrapping her arms around his neck and hanging on in sheer joy. Her body pressed to his, her breath touched his neck and he couldn't help but respond by wrapping his arms around her and holding her close.

"You did it," she said breathlessly. "I knew you could. I never doubted for a moment...well, maybe for a moment, but I really didn't have very many doubts about your..."

Sam turned his head; Lizzie turned hers. Their lips brushed, almost but not quite accidentally, and then he kissed her. After a brief second of surprise, she kissed him back.

Lizzie was warm and soft and giving. She tasted so good he didn't want to let her go—he didn't want to take his mouth from hers, not now, not ever. She kissed, not with practiced skill, but with wonder and gentleness and even curiosity. She held her breath. Her lips barely moved, but they did move. He felt that gentle movement shoot through him like a bolt of lightning that shook him from the top of his head to the bottoms of his feet. Lizzie must've felt it, too. She shuddered once, then melted in Sam's arms. Even though he knew it was a bad idea, he liked it. He liked it a lot.

Instinctively, she moved closer. Her body swayed into his; she pressed against him. The kiss deepened. It was time to stop; past time to stop. He was already imagining what it would be like to lay her across the desk and strip off those paint-stained ugly clothes that attempted, and failed, to hide a very fine body. He wanted her entirely naked, laid before him with a smile on her lips and all that warm, soft skin waiting for him.

The image in his mind spurred him on, and he deepened the kiss, getting lost in it. Sam never got lost, not anymore, but for a long moment he felt as if he were falling over the edge of a cliff, without control, without a care. The ground was rushing up toward him, and he didn't care. For a long, wonderful moment he didn't think about anything but the way holding and kissing Lizzie felt.

She was the one who ended the kiss, who slowly took her mouth from his and created a space between them, where before there had been none. "That was…that was…"

Nice? Amazing? Hot?

"That was a surprise." She brushed her hair back with one hand and looked away, suddenly shy. "I was just so excited to hear the news about getting close to Jenna, I couldn't help myself. Oh, wait, you kissed me first, didn't you? Were you excited, too?"

He supposed *excited* was a fitting enough word.

"For goodness' sake, Sam, do you kiss all your clients when a case is going well?" She tried to look at him, but her eyes didn't get any higher than his chest. "Shoot, I got a spot of paint on your shirt. Sorry. It won't come out. At least there's none on the jacket, not that I can see. Occupational hazard." Her gaze dropped. "There's a tiny spot on your pants, too. If we get right to it and scrub the paint out, maybe…"

She actually reached out as if she planned to brush

at the spot of paint on his upper thigh. *Not a good idea.* Sam's hand shot out and he grabbed her wrist. "Don't worry about it."

Don't worry about it. Ha! For nearly half of her life Lizzie had dreamed of kissing Sam Travers, and when that kiss had finally happened it had been everything she'd imagined, and more. He tasted and smelled so good, and his lips were soft, but not too soft. He'd held her tightly, but not too tightly—yes, the embrace that had accompanied the kiss had been just right, too. It was the kind of kiss that made the world stop spinning, for a while.

And now here they were. She was embarrassed and turned on and trembling in places she really should not tremble, and Sam had a hard-on he wasn't even attempting to hide. He could be a gentleman and turn around, or maybe grab a file folder off his desk and hold it strategically in front of him, but instead he just stood there.

The bottom had just dropped out of her world. She didn't know if she should be thrilled or terrified. In truth, she was a little bit of both. Sam had made it very clear that he liked being on his own. He didn't want to be tied down; he didn't want a woman who would call and ask where he was when he had to work late. He liked being alone; she didn't.

"I don't have casual sex," Lizzie said, her voice quick and uncertain. "Not that I haven't had the opportunity, some men do find me attractive and… But that's not the point. The point is, it seems kinda sad and icky to have sex with someone you barely know and maybe don't even like, though I suppose it could be…" She shook her head. "That's not the point, either. You're not a stranger at all. I'd say I know you as well as I know anyone else. And I do like you, I suppose you know that. The thing is, I'm not that girl."

"What girl?" he asked, his voice even and steady and sexy as hell.

"The girl that falls for a line and a really great kiss and ends up on her back and then the next day she wonders why the hell she didn't ask for more." Lizzie gathered the nerve to look up and into Sam's eyes. If she was ever going to have casual sex with anyone… No, she couldn't go there. "Maybe I don't have men lined up at my door, maybe it's been a couple of years since I had a serious boyfriend, but still, I deserve more than to be a quick lay in a long line of quick lays."

"I never said you didn't."

How could he be so calm? "Just so we're clear."

"Crystal."

She took a deep breath and changed the subject. "So, Thursday? Really? I'll have to finish painting your office before then. Not that it's a problem. Finishing up on Wednesday puts me right on schedule. I just don't want to get behind. I hate to leave a task unfinished."

There was a decidedly suggestive gleam in Sam's eyes as he responded. "So do I."

Her fantasies about Sam had always been just that. Fantasies. As a teenager she'd never *really* expected him to look at her one day and see her as a woman instead of a child. She'd never *really* expected him to leave Dottie Ann for the more worthy but much-too-young Lizzie. Those had made for very nice daydreams, but in reality Sam Travers had always been as far away from being hers as Brad Pitt was. And now here she was, still warm from kissing him. Still shaking. And right before her was clear evidence that he had not been unaffected. Fantasies were nice, but she had no illusions about the kind of man Sam was. She'd heard the words from his own mouth, just a few days ago. He liked being alone. He didn't want to be tied down by any woman.

Lizzie needed a forever guy. Someone who would stay, someone stable, someone who wanted marriage and kids and all that came with them. In an age when it wasn't all that popular, she was a fan of monogamy. Of commitment. She figured she had a better chance of snagging Brad Pitt or Johnny Depp than of turning Sam into the real, forever man she needed.

Pity. He did know how to kiss.

"You're staring at me," he said in a lowered voice.

"Am I?" she asked, not taking her eyes from his face.

"You are."

Trying to appear cool, feeling not at all cool, she reached up and patted his cheek. "You're awfully flushed and a little glassy-eyed. Bless your heart, do you need to sit down?"

In the past couple of years, Sam's duties had too often been more administrative than investigative. Sure, he still took assignments just as the other agents he employed did, and now and then a tricky job came along that he felt compelled to take on personally. But the truth was, a lot of paperwork came with the job now that the company had grown. He employed three full-time investigators and a receptionist, and there were a number of retired and out-of-town police officers who occasionally worked a job, if he needed the help and they could use a bit of cash.

Until Lizzie had asked him if he needed to "sit down"

because he was "flushed and a little glassy-eyed" after their kiss, he'd never felt old. With a few words and a pat on the cheek she made him feel as if he were hurtling toward retirement and unable to physically handle a little excitement.

Still, Sam was old enough and experienced enough to recognize when a woman was trying to push him away. He'd been pushed before; every man had. Wrong time, wrong woman, wrong place. The problem was, in spite of his earlier misgivings, he was pretty sure Lizzie wasn't the wrong woman. Wasn't that a kick in the pants? Neither of them was attached, so the problem couldn't be the timing. Wrong place? Maybe Lizzie thought he was crude enough to take her on top of his desk in the middle of a busy Monday while a handful of employees stood outside his office door. His unlocked door. Sure, he'd thought about it, but in truth he was a bit smoother than that. Usually.

She said she didn't do casual sex. There was a world of difference between a lifetime commitment and casual; there were many types of relationships in between. He wanted one with Lizzie, dammit, and he had a feeling there would be nothing casual about it.

He crept up behind her. Since she wore those earbuds again, he didn't even have to work very hard to remain silent. She jumped when he plucked one of the buds out of her ear, and then the other. He didn't want her to be distracted. He was standing close to her back, and a freshly painted wall was directly before her. She had nowhere to go. He grabbed her ponytail and wrapped it around his hand, then slowly bent forward to kiss the side of her neck. She didn't move. Didn't speak. If she told him to cut it out, he would. If she told him he wasn't her type, he'd back off. The problem was, Sam knew damn well he was Lizzie's type, just as she was his.

Her neck tasted sweet and salty and warm, and as he raked his lips across the sensitive skin there, she responded quickly with a shudder and a sigh. He moved his mouth to her nape and kissed her there. She trembled. Sam let go of Lizzie's ponytail and placed his hands on her hips, pulled her against him so she could feel how well they fit together. His hands circled her, held her as he moved his mouth to yet another part of her neck. She fell against him, nearing boneless.

Sam's hands slowly rose up Lizzie's torso to lightly brush the paint-spattered T-shirt that was stretched over small, firm breasts. His palms barely brushed her there. The nipples hardened and she gasped.

She remained oddly silent. The only sounds he heard were the muted and tinny strains of some popular love song echoing from the earbuds that hung down Lizzie's front along with the MP3 player, and her labored breathing.

After a few torturously long and wonderfully arousing moments, Sam dropped his hands and removed his mouth from Lizzie's skin. He backed away, one step and then two, and she spun on him.

This time she was the glassy-eyed one. Her cheeks were flushed; her lips were slightly parted.

"What the hell do you think you're doing?"

He gave her a grin. "Prep work."

Chapter 6

Lizzie was anxious for more reasons than one as she presented herself at the back door of the mansion where Jenna lived with her stepfather. She certainly could've gone in alone, would have preferred to go in alone, but Sam had been stubborn and would have none of it. He'd insisted on tagging along, as if he suspected she couldn't take care of herself in the simplest situation.

He hadn't touched her or made an inappropriate move since their disastrous encounter in his office a couple of days earlier. Since then she'd jumped at every unexpected sound, and she trembled at the timbre of Sam's voice, even when he said the most innocuous things. Even his less than appreciative "Okay, it doesn't look as bad as I thought it would" as he'd surveyed his newly painted office had sent shivers down her spine and had made her long to jump his bones. As if she needed encouragement.

Sam Travers made an excellent assistant, she supposed. He even looked the part in paint-stained jeans and a well-worn T-shirt topped with a loose button-up shirt. Gone was the smooth charmer whose expensive suits hid the weapons he insisted on carrying. She didn't kid herself about the too-large shirt he wore over his painter's duds. There was a weapon on his body, somewhere.

Today she'd chosen to wear her rattiest, baggiest, most paint-splattered overalls. She could've hidden her Taser, a couple of handguns and a full-length sword in the folds, if she was of a mind.

Jenna was at school, so as the housekeeper led Lizzie and Sam through the house, pointing out the rooms that needed to be painted, Lizzie didn't glance nervously around every corner. She didn't hold her breath. She studied the walls to be painted with her usual eye to detail. They weren't in horrible shape, not as Sam's office had been, but they could use a little loving care and a new coat of paint.

She didn't even argue when the housekeeper, Mrs. Scott, insisted that her employer wished the walls to remain the same, boring off-white they had always been. Since Lizzie wanted to stay low profile during this job, she'd give the customer exactly what he wanted, even if he was horribly wrong.

When they got to Jenna's room, at the far end of a wide hallway in the mansion's spacious second floor, Lizzie felt a shiver of a new and different kind of excitement. Beyond that door was the room of a girl who was probably her sister. The *probably* seemed less and less likely as days passed. Was it possible that the physical similarities were nothing more than coincidence? No, she didn't believe so. Maybe she should find a sneaky way to do a DNA test without Jenna ever knowing.

An unpleasant jolt shot through Lizzie's body. The test would take time, Sam had already told her, and she wanted answers now. Besides, if the test came back negative, it would break her heart. Maybe she didn't really want to know....

Jenna's walls were painted a gentle, pale yellow. The room was sunny and girlish, the special place of a spoiled princess who had everything she might ever ask for. The furniture was white and looked outrageously expensive. There was a white net canopy draped over the bed, falling in waves over a floral-print bedspread in yellow, green and lavender. There were pictures everywhere. One was of a little girl and the woman Lizzie remembered as Monica Yates. Others showed an older Jenna with friends, her stepfather, holding a trophy...

"Jenna would like to choose her own paint color," the housekeeper said, already leading Lizzie and Sam from the room. "She'll be home this afternoon, after soccer practice."

"I have some color samples in my truck," Lizzie said as she stepped once more into the boring, off-white hallway. "Perhaps we can meet with Jenna when she gets home and go over some of the options." Her heart thumped as she said the words, forcing herself to remain calm in demeanor. Just a few more hours, and she'd see Jenna face-to-face.

The housekeeper nodded, already bored and obviously ready to get back to her normal duties. If she realized that Sam was the man behind the bribe that had coerced her to insist to her employer that it was time for the interiors to be repainted, she didn't show it in any way. Not that Lizzie thought for a moment that Sam would've made the offer himself. No, he had people for that sort of thing.

She glanced at him as they walked to the truck to collect supplies. He'd hung back so far, letting her do all the talking. Who in their right mind would believe that he worked for her? Even in his less than magnificent clothing, he looked like a leader. This was a man accustomed to being in charge, and that was tough to hide. Goodness knows she'd do anything he told her to do! Well, almost anything.

As much as she'd fantasized about him for all these years, she'd never *ever* dreamed of actually sleeping with him.

"Scoot on out of here," she said as casually as she could manage. "Take the truck. You can pick me up at five-thirty."

Sam reached into the bed of the truck and easily lifted out her toolbox. "No," he said simply and decisively.

"This is hardly dangerous duty," she argued, opening the door and reaching into the backseat for a roll of plastic. "I'm sure you have more important things to do."

"What do you think will happen if Connelly finds out you bribed your way into the house?"

"He won't," she argued. "And even if he did, the only thing he could do is kick me out."

Sam made a snorting sound and moved toward the back door with his hands full. "There are a lot of twisted people in the world. You never know when you might run into one."

She scurried behind him. "If you thought Connelly was twisted, you wouldn't have tried to convince me that Jenna is better off not knowing the truth."

"I have no evidence, and odds are he's the upstanding citizen he appears to be."

"So, you'll play the odds with Jenna but not with me?"

Sam twisted his head and looked at her, hard. "Jenna isn't my responsibility."

"Neither am I!" Lizzie increased her step to catch up with him.

She could barely hear him as he responded, "Yeah, you are, dammit."

This was not his usual sort of case. Not even close. Sam moved furniture, laid drop cloth, sanded where he was told to sand and puttied small holes. They started the job in what the housekeeper called the South Parlor, a large square room with floor-to-ceiling windows facing the front lawn and heavy walnut furniture that looked much older than the house itself. The framed paintings on the walls were oils that looked to be expensive, but Sam didn't pretend to know anything about art. These landscapes and still lifes hadn't been picked up at the semiannual starving artists show, he imagined.

There were no family pictures anywhere, not in this room. Anyone might've lived here. Unlike Jenna's bedroom, this room had no character at all. It was lifeless, soulless, sterile, like a picture out of a magazine.

And as instructed, Lizzie would repaint the walls the same dull off-white, though he imagined she'd cheat a little bit and bypass the generic off-white for a moonlight cream or heirloom lace. She'd give the room a little touch of life, whether Connelly wanted it or not.

Shortly before noon, Darryl Connelly and his lady friend arrived, pulling into the driveway just beyond the sunlit windows, rushing to the front door laughing. They entered the house and as they passed the parlor, the woman asked Darryl what was going on.

"Painters," he said simply. "Mary told me it was time to freshen up the walls, and I suppose she knows what she's talking about. What's the point in having a full-time housekeeper if you don't let her do her job?"

The woman barely glanced into the room, and when she did, she didn't bother to look at the two workmen there. Instead she wrinkled her nose at the mess, and then they disappeared down a long hallway.

People like these never gave the common man the time of day. The painters were invisible, just like the gardener and the housekeeper. That was a good thing, considering their mission here.

"Lunch," Sam said simply, setting his putty knife aside and tightly covering the small tub of putty.

"Are you hungry?" Lizzie asked as she set aside her block sander.

"Starving."

They walked out the back door and to her truck, where an ice chest held cold sodas and bottled water, and a plastic bag of sandwiches and chips sat behind the seat. The food Lizzie had brought with her wasn't fancy, but there was plenty of it. They could've gone some-where for a bite, he supposed, but now that she was here she didn't want to leave until she saw Jenna. He under-stood that. She was so close.

Sam jumped into the back of the truck and offered

Lizzie a hand. She took it, and he helped her up and in. Once there, they sat with their backs to the cab, legs stretched out, food sitting between them.

He'd decided days ago—right after the kiss, to be specific—that he was going to have Lizzie, but he hadn't decided exactly how or when. She wasn't a woman to be smoothly seduced and then dismissed. She wasn't likely to agree to the logical argument that they were both unattached and healthy and attracted, so why not have a little fun? He wouldn't tell her that he wanted everything she did, because that would be a lie. He lied every day, in his line of work, but he wouldn't lie to her. She deserved better. She deserved more than he could ever give her.

That didn't leave many options. It was very possible there were no options at all. At least, none that would satisfy everyone involved.

"You're too quiet," he said, glancing across to the woman at his side. She'd cocked one knee up and seemed to be enjoying her lunch well enough. She'd probably eaten lunch like this a thousand times, with warm, fresh air on her face and her muscles welcoming the rest.

"I'm too wound up to talk," she said, and then she smiled. "Lucky you."

Might as well make light of the situation. "I'm just afraid once you see Jenna you'll explode, and then so much for our cover."

"I do know how to hold my tongue when it's necessary," she said. "No matter what, I don't plan to drop the truth on Jenna like a bombshell."

"Good."

He wondered what Lizzie would do when she saw for herself that Jenna was happy and safe. Maybe Darryl

Connelly wasn't the warmest stepfather in the world, but Sam had spent a lot of time digging into the man's personal life. Connelly had been watched for the better part of the past week. There were no signs of drug or alcohol abuse, and certainly no indication of child endangerment. True, the man was much more taken with his current girlfriend, Heather Mann, than he was with his preteen stepdaughter, but that didn't make him a bad person. Connelly, for all his faults, had stepped up to the plate after his wife's death and had become father to a child who wasn't biologically his. Who could find fault with that?

Sam had a feeling Lizzie would need him more after this job was done than she did now. Once she knew Jenna was better off here, ignorant of her potential connection to Lizzie, she'd be devastated. He had no doubt that she would do what was best for the child, but it would hurt her more than she knew. She wasn't prepared for that kind of heartbreak.

He'd spoken to a couple of labs that did paternity work, and the word he'd gotten so far wasn't good. Given the possible relationship between Lizzie and Jenna, they preferred blood or saliva for comparison. It wasn't as if they could swipe the kid's toothbrush and get a definite answer. He hadn't told Lizzie yet, but then, she wasn't pushing for a test. Not yet.

"What are you doing tonight?" he asked.

Lizzie's head snapped around and she glared at him. "Nothing. There's a movie on television I'd like to see, and I'm thinking of making a tuna salad for tomorrow's lunch. I have a couple loads of laundry to do, and if I feel like it I might bake some cookies."

"That's an awful lot of nothing," he said, leaning

slightly toward her. "How about you forget all that and go out to dinner with me. A good steak, a bottle of wine, maybe something chocolate for dessert."

Lizzie leaned slightly away from him, her eyes narrowing. "Is this more prep work?" she asked suspiciously.

"A man's gotta eat."

Her cheeks flushed, nice and pink. Her hazel eyes sparkled. This close he could see every color, every speck of green and lightning strike of gold. There was life in those eyes. "I guess I could save my laundry for tomorrow night," she said softly.

Sam looked her up and down. She was sexy as hell in baggy clothes and no makeup and not a speck of jewelry. All dolled up she would likely kill him. But man, what a way to go. "Wear a dress," he said, and then he backed away from her and gave all his attention to the sandwich in his hand.

The last thing she needed was something else to worry about! Dinner with Sam; a dream come true. Literally. Was this going to be a date? Did he think it was a date? He wanted her to wear a dress, and since he'd asked her out he looked at her as if he wanted to eat her up. It all added up to *date* in her mind. She'd told him very clearly what she wanted, and still he persisted. They didn't want the same things from life. Well, they did, in a very basic way, but her idea of a relationship and his were miles apart. One of them was going to fold. The way her heart was beating, she suspected it might be her.

Maybe one night with the man of her dreams would be enough to hold her for a while. Maybe he'd make an ass of himself and she'd learn the hard way that he wasn't Mr. Perfect after all.

She could only hope. As if it wasn't bad enough that she already compared every man she met to him! If Sam was a great date and a fabulous lover, she'd be ruined for life. Then again, if he was a "slam, bam, thank you, ma'am" kinda guy, she could count herself lucky that he wasn't into permanent relationships. Something to ponder…

Pondering did make the afternoon fly by quickly. From her position near the windows in the South Parlor of the Connelly home she heard the car pull into the driveway. She looked at a nearby clock. Four-forty. She looked through the windows and held her breath as Jenna exited the car, backpack slung over one shoulder, wide smile on her pretty, Charlie-like face. She was wearing shorts and a T-shirt, and was mussed and a little sweaty, having just come from soccer practice.

"Steady, now," Sam said calmly. "Don't attack the girl as she comes in the door."

"I won't," she snapped, glaring at him. He had no faith in her at all! And then he smiled, and she knew that he did have faith in her. He just knew her a little too well. She was about to explode!

Jenna came in the front door, slamming it behind her. Connelly came out of his office, made his way to the front of the house and met Jenna with a casual smile.

"The painters are here!" Jenna said brightly, stepping into the parlor with a wide smile that matched the voice. Unlike her stepfather and his girlfriend, who'd left hours ago, she looked directly at Lizzie and Sam. "All day I've been trying to decide what color I want to paint my room. Lavender, maybe, or blue. Not pink, I did decide that much, and not yellow again. I'm ready for a new color."

Lizzie very calmly put her sander aside and walked toward Jenna. This close, she could see that the girl's eyes were the same shade of hazel as her own—eyes like her father's. Their father's? The similarities she'd seen from a distance were more pronounced up close. Did Jenna really look so much like Charlie, or was that wishful thinking?

"I brought some paint samples with me," Lizzie said. "Maybe we can go through them in your room. With the light there and your things all around we'll be able to get a better idea of how the colors will work."

"Cool." Jenna headed for the stairway, and Lizzie followed. She was immediately aware that Sam was right behind her.

She stopped in the parlor entrance and spun to face him. "Homer, you can finish puttying the nail holes in the molding. That way we can start painting the trim tomorrow." Sam glared at her so fiercely she was glad of the opportunity to face Darryl Connelly. "Whoever painted this room the first time around didn't have much of an eye for detail. There were quite a number of unfilled nail holes and rough patches on the wall. Homer is new at this, but he's learning." She lowered her voice slightly. "He might not be the brightest crayon in the box, but he's a hard worker."

Sam couldn't just keep his mouth shut and do as he was told. Oh, no. "Prep work is very important, or so Miss Porter tells me."

Lizzie glanced back at Sam as she and Jenna headed up the stairs and Connelly returned to his office. Her "helper" was annoyed and amused. It was likely no one surprised him these days. And while he probably took on many aliases in his line of work, he'd probably never been Homer, the not-so-bright painter's assistant. He smiled at her and nodded, and she smiled back.

Jenna led Lizzie to her room, throwing open the door and tossing her book bag onto the bed. "What do you think? Lavender or blue? Not a dark blue, something light and pretty, but not too light, I don't want a pastel color. Something in between dark and light. Is Homer your boyfriend? He works for you and he called you Miss Porter, but he's cute and he looked at you like you were a girlfriend, but that's really none of my business." She took a deep breath and brushed a long strand of mussed hair away from her face. "What do you think? Blue or lavender?"

"Personally, I prefer blue, but let's look at some color samples." Lizzie pulled a stack of color cards out of her back pocket and laid them on the bed, scattering them out and plucking out the ones that wouldn't suit. Having had a look at Jenna's room that morning, she knew what colors the girl would prefer, and there were several samples in the shades Jenna had mentioned.

"How was school?" Lizzie asked casually as she plucked out the colors which were too light or too dark.

"Pretty good," Jenna said as she studied the colors. "Except that my math teacher is a psycho."

"Psycho?"

"Only a psycho would assign so much homework. This one." Jenna plucked out a color chip in Aegean blue.

"I like it," Lizzie said. She wanted to take Jenna by the shoulders and look her in the eye and ask, "Are you happy? Does Connelly take good care of you? Do you have lots of friends at school? You're too young for a boyfriend, but is there a boyfriend? Oh, please tell me there's no boyfriend yet."

Instead she looked as casually as possible at the child and realized that Sam had been right all along. This girl had everything. She was well cared for. She lacked for nothing—except perhaps a sister. Maybe when she was grown she'd like to know that she had a sister. Maybe when she was eighteen or twenty or thirty they could talk about paternity tests and possibilities. But for now—Jenna didn't need Lizzie in her life. Revealing what she knew would only turn the child's neat life upside down.

Lizzie snatched up the paint sample. "When we finish downstairs we'll start here. It'll probably be this weekend or early next week." Even though the contract was for several rooms, when Jenna's room was done she'd move on. It wasn't as though she planned to charge Connelly for work she didn't do, and to stay here for several more days and keep her mouth shut would be difficult. More than that, it would hurt—more than she'd imagined.

"Nice," Jenna said, and then she plopped down on the bed to open her backpack and dig inside, probably for the math homework.

In the doorway, Lizzie stopped and turned to face Jenna one more time. For all she knew this would be her last close look for a long while. "This is a very nice room," she said. "You're a lucky girl."

Jenna shrugged her shoulders. "Yeah, I guess so." Her head snapped up. "So, is Homer your boyfriend or not?"

Lizzie gave the girl a soft smile and fought tears. "It's too early to say. I'll let you know."

Chapter 7

Sam pulled into Lizzie's driveway at seven on the dot. He'd showered and gladly tossed his painter's clothes into the hamper, exchanging them for a navy blue suit.

Homer. Lizzie owed him big-time for that one. He'd used plenty of false names in his career as a P.I., but Homer? Never. Annoyed as he was, he couldn't help but smile. There was never a dull moment when Lizzie was around.

After she'd spent some time with Jenna, Lizzie hadn't had much to say. She'd been quiet on the drive back to the office. Sam hadn't pushed for details, because he'd known all along how this would go. Jenna was a happy, normal kid, and to turn her world upside down would be cruel. Lizzie wasn't cruel. With any luck she'd be satisfied knowing her sister was in good hands. Maybe she'd found some comfort in meeting the girl, even though they couldn't know one another well. Not yet, at least. When Jenna was grown, the truth could come out without causing too much drama. Maybe.

Child custody investigations were the worst. Every time he got involved in one, Sam was doubly happy that he and Dottie Ann had never had children. As if either of them needed to procreate…

Sam ran up the three steps to Lizzie's tiny front porch and rang the doorbell. He waited. For a long moment all was silent, and he wondered if she'd even remembered their date. A lot had happened since their shared lunch in the back of her truck.

Finally he heard footsteps. Slow, steady footsteps. The latch was undone, and the doorknob turned. The door swung open on Lizzie.

She had not forgotten.

Sam tried not to let his surprise show. He was usually pretty good at hiding his reactions, but Lizzie's half smile told him he hadn't succeeded this time. She cleaned up nicely. Very nicely.

Her little black dress fit her just so. The cut of the dress showed off her delicate but decidedly shapely figure. She wore makeup, but not too much, and there were sparkly diamond studs in her ears. Her chestnut hair was down, softly curling, thick and silky. There was no sloppy ponytail for her tonight, no paint-stained work clothes. She wore a pair of black spike heels that made her legs go on forever.

Lizzie no longer bore any resemblance to the little girl he remembered. She was fully grown, beautiful and tempting.

But some things never changed.

"Fair warning, I'm going to seduce you tonight," she

said, closing the door behind her and hiking her black shoulder bag into a more comfortable position. "Well, I'm going to try, anyway. You're difficult about everything else, so I suppose you'll be difficult about this, too. Anyway, unless you're a horrible date and I change my mind between now and when you bring me home, I'm going to give it my best shot." She cast him a wary and incredibly sexy glance. "I'm new at the whole seduction thing, so be kind."

Sam wanted to ask Lizzie why she'd changed her mind, but he knew. The chemistry between them was strong, and it grew more potent every minute they spent together. It would be a waste to walk away from something that was sure to be dynamite just because they had a few fundamental differences.

If she wanted to seduce him, he sure as hell wasn't going to try to stop her.

Dinner was lovely. Sam ordered steak. Lizzie ordered salmon. Both came with a fabulous salad, rolls and potato. She was sure it was all wonderful. If only she'd been able to taste her food.

It had seemed easier to be up-front with Sam about what she wanted, but her blunt statement about seduction hung between them as they ate and chatted, talking about nothing of importance as the minutes dragged on with unbearable lethargy. Sam occasionally looked at her as if he wanted her here and now, on the table, the other diners be damned. Seducing him was going to be much too easy.

And now Sam was delivering her home, as any proper date would. He pulled into her driveway and turned off the engine, jumped out of the car and hurried to her side to open the door like a real gentleman, as if they were on a date. They actually were on a date, she supposed. They'd dressed the part. He'd insisted on paying. He'd driven her home. And within a very short period of time she planned to be very naked.

She hadn't changed her mind about the sadness of casual sex, but if what she felt when she looked at Sam was any indication, there was nothing casual about this. Maybe he didn't want the kind of relationship she did, but that didn't mean they couldn't have *something*. In his case, she was willing to compromise. She'd rather have some of Sam than nothing at all.

On the way to the door he placed his hand on the small of her back, and she shuddered. A quiver worked its way up her spine, from the place he touched her to her nape. The air changed when he was close to her. It grew thicker and heavier and more alive. There was electricity in the air when Sam was near, electricity she could feel and taste. Maybe that was why she felt as though she was about to pop.

Should she offer him coffee and ease her way into seduction with a few meaningful glances and a sexy laugh or two? Jump his lovely bones the minute they walked in the door? Just walk toward the bedroom, stripping as she went and hoping he'd follow? She'd worn her best black bra and matching panties, and they wouldn't look too horrible draped across the stairs, she imagined. Seduction was not her strong suit. Maybe she wasn't a virgin, exactly, but her past experiences had been rushed and clumsy and had pretty much just happened—and had only reinforced that she wasn't one for just being casual. She didn't want Sam to just "happen." She wanted tonight to be special. He wanted her now; she knew that. But after he'd had her once, would he be finished with her? She didn't fool herself into thinking that he was going to suddenly transform into a forever kind of guy just because they had sex. She didn't expect declarations of love and marriage proposals because he was so stunned and overwhelmed by her body.

So, what did she expect?

Lizzie unlocked the front door and stepped inside, turning on the foyer light almost automatically. "Coffee?"

"No." Sam's voice absolutely rumbled, it was so low.

Plan number one, down. Lizzie turned to face him. She really wasn't a strip seductively on the way to the bedroom kinda girl, even if she was wearing her good underwear. That didn't leave her many options.

She lifted her head to look Sam in the eye, and as she did he lowered his head to kiss her. It was natural; it was simple. No planning necessary. The kiss just happened, as if they were instinctively drawn together. Sam didn't just kiss her; he claimed her mouth, he made her melt. With a flick of his tongue and a hand on her hip, he turned her into a spineless jellyfish. Sensations that made her earlier quiver look like child's play seeped through her entire body, until she felt as if she had no will and was simply flying toward the inevitable.

This is the way it should be, she thought as she drifted into him, lost in his warmth and great kiss.

"Wait a minute," she said, taking her mouth from his with great reluctance. "*I'm* supposed to be seducing *you*."

"You've been seducing me all night," he said, leading her into the living room, slipping her purse off her shoulder and deftly tossing it aside. "That dress, the way you smile, the curve of your neck, the way you plucked at your skirt in the car as we got closer to the house…all seduction."

"I had no idea those little things could be considered seduction," Lizzie said, and her mouth went dry.

Sam sighed. "Neither did I." He sat on the couch and pulled her onto his lap. She did not land gracefully, but lost her balance at the last second and landed pretty hard. He caught her, held her, guided her into a leaning position and began to kiss her throat. One hand slid slowly up her thigh, just barely slipping under her skirt and then stopping. Now, *this* was seduction.

Her earlier dismissal of casual sex seemed rather silly, as Sam held and kissed and touched her. This was so good, so powerful…she felt almost like another woman. A lucky woman. A woman who wouldn't over-think such a beautiful moment in her life.

Yes, it was very nice, but Lizzie kept waiting for Sam to go for the gold, to scoot that warm hand farther up her leg and get rid of the panties that were in the way. Did he expect to get busy right here on the couch? That didn't make much sense with a perfectly good bed just up the stairs.

His hand inched upward, very slightly. She took in a deep breath and held it.

"Relax," he whispered.

Was he kidding? Relaxing was never easy for her, and *now?* No way. "I don't think I can."

"Too wound up?" His mouth trailed down between her breasts.

Lizzie trembled. "You could say that." *Wound up* was hardly the proper phrase. *About to explode* was more accurate. She'd been on the edge of detonation all

day, for one reason or another. Sam was about to push
her over the edge. She had a fuse; he had a flame.

"I have the cure for that," he said, a confident statement that did absolutely nothing to ease her tension.
Nothing at all.

Lizzie had planned to be in control tonight. She'd
planned to be the one doing the seducing. She'd figured
that one way or another she'd have Sam salivating over
her before they finally did the deed. And here she was,
entirely at his mercy.

She couldn't think, she couldn't even breathe
properly, and they were both still completely dressed.

His hand inched a little higher, and her legs instinctively parted, ever so slightly. Her heart skipped a beat,
her stomach did a flip and low in her belly she felt a
heaviness that drove out every other thought, every
other need. All she could think about was that hand and
where it was going… There was no room in her brain
for a single other thought.

"I have a perfectly good bed right up the…"

"Not yet," Sam said, shifting his body and hers as he
reached well between her thighs and too-quickly and
too-lightly massaged her through the thin silk panties.

The little noise deep in her throat caught Lizzie by
surprise. It was a moan and a groan and a plea, all
wrapped into one soft sound of desperation and need.
Her heart pounded; the room swam. And all the while
Sam touched her. She was too quickly at his mercy, too
soon putty in his very capable hands. Maybe this wasn't
what she'd planned, exactly, but she wasn't about to
complain. If she did, he might stop, and that would never
do.

Moving slowly, too slowly, he slipped her panties off

and down. An inch at a time, his fingers trailing her skin, the black panties were removed and dropped aside. If he wanted to have her here on the couch, that was fine with her. Maybe the bed was too far away to suit him. At the moment it seemed awfully far away to her.

His mouth latched to hers; she did love the way he kissed. His tongue slipped into her mouth and his hand moved between her legs in a gentle rhythm that matched the kiss. She found herself moving against him, her hips rocking. She was driven by a physical need so strong it wiped away everything else. There was nothing but Sam and need and the promise of what was to come. When he slipped a finger inside her, she gasped and clutched him close. He teased her, once, twice, and she orgasmed so hard she cried out. Her body jerked as the sensations of release whipped through her.

Too soon. Too fast. Too amazing…

He lifted his body slightly from hers and smiled down at her. "Now you're relaxed."

Lizzie looked into Sam's fine blue eyes, she studied the smile and the truth wiped away what remained of the bliss. He'd made her come and now he was going to walk away. She was a total failure as a seductress. "That wasn't exactly what I had in mind."

"We're not finished," he said, and his eyes narrowed. "Take off your dress before I rip it off."

Now, *that* was more like it.

She was more relaxed than she'd been when they'd first come to the couch, she'd give him that much. Actually, she was more relaxed than she'd been in days! Weeks. Had she ever felt so good? Lizzie lay back on the couch and smiled. "You first."

"I'm not wearing a dress."

"You know what I mean." She waved her fingers at him. "Remove that suit."

Sam slipped off his jacket and tossed it aside, and Lizzie's eyes were immediately drawn to the shoulder holster and gun he wore. Her smile faded and her eyes narrowed.

"You were wearing that gun the whole time? All through dinner? When you made me come? That's just *wrong,* Sam."

He plucked the weapon from its holster and put it on the end table. "Sorry. I pretty much wear it all the time."

"Not when you're with me, not like this," she said, and then she added, "Please."

He removed the leather holster strap and dropped it near the jacket. "You're still dressed," he said.

Lizzie made herself more comfortable on the couch. "So are you."

"Where's that bed you were telling me about?" He offered her a hand and she took it. He tugged gently and she stood.

And the world exploded.

Not the world, precisely, but her living room was, without warning, a war zone. The front windows shattered. The blast of a gun filled the air, then another. Somewhere between the shots, Sam tackled her. His reflexes were great, she'd give him that much. Before her mind could process what was happening, he had her on the floor, his long, hot body protecting hers.

She found herself oddly relieved that they were not yet naked.

At the squealing of tires Sam jumped up, ordered her to stay put and grabbed his gun. He rushed out the front door. How could she stay put when Sam was rushing toward the gunfire instead of away from it? She did stay low as she crawled toward the door, only to arrive as Sam came back inside.

"I told you to stay put," he said, but there was no anger in his voice.

"They're gone?"

"Yeah. I didn't even get a look at the car."

He snagged his cell phone from his belt and dialed 911. He reported gunshots fired as if he were still on the force, and then he closed and locked the front door and helped her to her feet. "I'm sorry," he said as he led her back to the couch, where there would be no more hanky-panky tonight, she suspected. Gunshots were a major mood killer.

"It's not your fault," she said, snagging her panties from the floor and shoving them behind a couch cushion as she heard sirens approaching already. That was fast.

"How many people want you dead?" he asked sharply.

"None. At least, none that I know of." Painters were never high on anyone's hit list.

"I can't say the same, though this is a first even for me. Dammit, Lizzie, I'm sorry I dragged you into this." He put his shoulder holster in place and dropped his gun where it belonged.

Gone was the man who had smiled at her and touched her with perfection and ordered her to disrobe. Gone was the man who had promised her "more."

She didn't think she was nearly adept enough at seduction to bring that man back.

Chapter 8

Sam rarely got truly angry these days. The emotion wasn't productive and in fact often caused normally reasonable men to make stupid mistakes they could never walk away from.

But tonight he was angry. What had he been thinking? Apparently he couldn't make Lizzie a part of his world, not even for one night, without putting her in harm's way. She deserved better. Hell, any decent woman deserved better than to be sucked into his life, so where did that leave him?

Free as a bird, which is what he wanted to be. Right?

Truthfully, while his job came with its dangers he wasn't exactly a walking target. There had been confrontations, sure, but he'd never before been shot at. He wouldn't knowingly put any woman in danger. He was overreacting, looking for logic where there was none.

Knowing that didn't ease his anger. Neither did knowing that it would've been impossible for the shooter to see into the house, to know that his bullets had come so close.

Lizzie had finally gone to bed—alone—around two in the morning, after the cops had left and Danny had arrived. Together Sam and Danny had boarded up the shattered windows—with help from a carpenter friend—and they'd set the police on Skinner as the most likely suspect. He was, at least, the most recent trouble-maker. Not that there weren't others who held a grudge. Working child custody cases, investigating murders and looking for people who didn't want to be found brought a lot of angry people into Sam's circle.

Lizzie had used her Taser on Skinner on their first and only meeting. A reasonable man would be grateful that she'd saved him from being shot, but Skinner, the inept insurance fraud, was anything but reasonable. She'd told him she was the painter, so it wouldn't have been impossible for him to find her. Someone could've followed Sam; someone might've tracked down Lizzie. Either way, Sam had gone from being turned on to royally pissed in a relatively short period of time.

He and Danny stood in Lizzie's driveway. At this hour of the morning the neighborhood was quiet. The front window was boarded up. Lizzie was asleep—or should be. In a couple of hours, dawn would arrive, and arrangements would have to be made. Danny was smart enough to keep quiet, to do as he was told and not ask too many questions, and he was also observant enough to realize that this was far from a normal case.

Sam leaned against his own car, trying to unwind. It wasn't happening. Hours had passed and he could still feel Lizzie beneath him, still smell her, still hear those little sounds she made, sounds that revealed the depth of her response. He wanted her more than he'd ever wanted anything, and he wouldn't have her. Not tonight. Not ever.

Much as it sucked at the moment, he'd get over it. He'd forget how she felt and smelled and sighed, and he'd get on with his life. She needed to get on with hers.

Without looking at Danny, he said, "Tomorrow you're going to play painter's assistant."

"I am?"

"Yeah. I want Lizzie watched 24/7 until we know who fired that shot."

"Gotcha." Danny looked toward the house. "I like her," he said, his voice lowered in homage to the night. "She's funny as hell even when she doesn't intend to be, and she's definitely not your average female, but there's something about her that's charming. She's pretty, but she doesn't priss around like a lot of beautiful girls do. Nice ass, too."

"You like her so much, ask her out," Sam said, a trace of that anger he tried to suppress in his voice.

"I thought you and her were...you know."

"Nope." Couldn't be. Wouldn't work. Not even for one night, dammit. "Her father and I were partners for a few years, a long time ago." Danny was closer to Lizzie's age. He was a good kid, but he had chosen the same dangerous profession that made it impossible for Sam to think seriously about getting involved. How could he tell Danny that he wasn't good enough for Lizzie, two seconds after he'd told him to feel free to ask her out?

"I would take her out to dinner or a movie and see where it took us," Danny said, "but I've been seeing this girl kinda regular and I don't want to mess it up."

Sam felt a rush of relief. Maybe he couldn't claim Lizzie, but he didn't want to stand around and watch someone else do it, either. Eventually someone would. Some lucky man would snatch her up and treat her the way she deserved to be treated. She should have that, and more, but he didn't want to watch. He was going to have to take care of her case and then get rid of her.

Somehow he was sure that wouldn't be easy.

Lizzie wasn't surprised to find Danny waiting for her as she headed for the truck. Disappointed, yes, but not surprised. He'd dressed in appropriate clothes for painting, and wore a friendly smile. He was an attractive man, dark-haired like Sam but with really dark eyes. Danny wasn't as tall as Sam, but he had a nice, muscular build, the kind a lot of women went for.

Even though she'd pretty much expected that Sam would back off as much as possible, after last night's excitement—the excitement that had happened when someone had shot at her, not the more pleasant excitement she'd been enjoying beforehand—she was disheartened. Something special danced just out of reach where she and Sam were concerned. She felt it so strongly it was almost palpable. They could have something so special, so wonderful, if only he'd let it happen.

But she smiled for Danny and pushed her disappointment deep. "You're my assistant for the day?"

"Yep. Sam had a bunch of other stuff to do today, but after last night he didn't want to send you out alone."

"I hardly think there's any danger at the Connelly house."

Danny shrugged his shoulders and jumped into the passenger seat. "Probably not. Lucky for you I'm also good at heavy lifting and I take orders well. I haven't painted in a while, but I'm no virgin, either. And I really like the color you chose for the boss's office, even if it is pink."

"It's cinnamon taupe," she said.

"That's what Sam tells me."

They rode most of the way in comfortable silence. Danny stared out the window, and Lizzie's mind spun about madly, torn between finding and perhaps claiming her sister and the predicament with Sam. Why couldn't the person who'd shot at them arrive half an hour later? Judging by the look on Sam's face the last time she'd seen him, as he'd sent her to bed as though she was still a little girl, there wouldn't be a second chance.

They arrived at the Connelly house, and Lizzie pulled her truck around back, parking in the same spot she had yesterday. An ancient oak tree shaded the cab. Since Sam wasn't here, she'd concentrate on Jenna and that predicament. One disastrous relationship at a time...

The kitchen door was unlocked, and after knocking and yelling hello, they walked into the house. In one trip she and Danny managed to carry in almost all that they'd need to finish in the parlor. Lizzie was already planning ahead. When the parlor was done, she'd paint Jenna's room and then move on. In her heart she knew it was best that she walk away, for now, but it was going to be difficult.

She'd started this episode in her life with no sister and no Sam, and it looked as if it was going to end that way. So, why did she feel more alone than she had when she'd begun?

On their second and final trip into the house, Darryl Connelly met Lizzie and Danny at the back door, a tight smile on his face. His eyes were bloodshot as if he'd been crying—or drinking excessively. Or simply not sleeping well. "Good morning, Miss Porter."

She was a little taken aback that he knew her name, and then she realized that he'd been the one to write her a deposit check yesterday, before she'd left. And Sam had called her Miss Porter, at least once. Duh. "Good morning, Mr. Connelly," she said evenly, keeping a businesslike tone to her voice.

Connelly's eyes flitted over her shoulder. "I see you have a new helper today. What happened to Homer?"

Danny started to laugh then faked a cough that covered it well.

"I'm afraid Homer is no longer with me. He was offered a better job elsewhere, so my cousin Floyd offered to help me out. I hope you don't mind."

"Not at all," Connelly said smoothly. He held the back door open for her and for Danny, and then followed them into the parlor.

The hairs on Lizzie's neck stood up. Connelly hadn't paid her or Sam any mind at all yesterday, and today he was escorting her and Danny into the house as if they were guests, not workmen. It wasn't right. Lizzie strained to listen, but the house was much too quiet. Where was the housekeeper? Jenna would be at school, but what about Connelly's airhead girlfriend who was here so often? Why did the house feel like a tomb?

As she carefully placed her paint can on a sheet of plastic in the parlor, she turned to face Connelly. Yes, he was watching her much too closely.

"Where is Mrs. Scott this morning?" Lizzie asked.

Connelly's eyebrows rose slightly. "Oh, yes, Mary was the one who recommended you for this job, wasn't she?"

"Yes."

"I'm afraid she's found a better-paying job elsewhere, much like your Homer."

Lizzie's stomach plummeted. Suddenly she felt as if a rock had taken up residence there. "That's too bad."

"Yes, she was quite competent."

Competent. What a raving review.

"I'm hoping you can finish up the job no later than Sunday afternoon," Connelly said crisply. "Tomorrow would be best."

"Of course."

"My daughter, Jenna, will be spending the weekend with a friend. I thought it best that she not be exposed to noxious paint fumes."

Lizzie's heart sank. She knew she needed to keep her distance, had come to that decision all on her own, but in truth she'd looked forward to seeing Jenna over the weekend. Maybe it was better this way. "That's understandable. I'll just check with her this afternoon to make sure she hasn't changed her mind about the color..."

"I'm afraid Jenna won't be here this afternoon," Connelly interrupted. "She'll be going to her friend's house directly from school. Feel free to paint the room in whatever color she chose yesterday. If she doesn't like it I'll repaint the room myself." He smiled tightly, his bloodshot eyes hardened and locked to hers. "Nothing is too good for my little girl."

The room spun a little. The world tilted. Connelly knew. Somehow, he knew who Lizzie was and why she was here. He wouldn't confront her, wouldn't admit that he knew who she was and kick her out, but she could see the truth in his eyes and in the tight set of his mouth. For the first time in a long while Lizzie was at a loss for words. Her mouth went dry; her heart pounded so hard she wondered if Connelly and Danny could hear it. Where was Sam? She needed him here. He would know what to do, what to say. In the end she didn't have to come up with a response. Connelly turned and walked away, leaving her to do her work.

And still, she couldn't move.

"Are you okay?" Danny asked softly.

Lizzie lied. "Yes, I'm fine. I just didn't get enough sleep last night."

"I hear ya," he said, and then he started unpacking rollers and paintbrushes, getting ready for what would surely be the longest day of Lizzie's life.

Jim Skinner had an airtight alibi for last night when the shots had been fired into Lizzie's living room— he'd still been in jail—which put Sam back at square one. If the man Lizzie had used her Taser on hadn't been the one to shoot at her house, then who? Someone who'd followed Sam there, no doubt. He had Marilyn pull the files from his nastiest cases, and he was going through each file, searching for the man—or woman— who would fire blindly into a house where two people were ignorantly getting busy on the couch.

Someone who had a history of turning to violence. Someone who'd made threats. He ended up with a short list of suspects that would take days—maybe weeks— to properly investigate.

Until he knew what had happened and why, Lizzie would remain under guard. Not by him, though. He didn't trust himself with her, not after the way he'd lost control last night. What had he been thinking? The little head had taken over again. He was always screwed whenever that happened.

Sam leaned back in his chair and looked at the picture of him and Charlie after that last fishing trip, a picture which hung on a cinnamon taupe wall. For a while he'd been determined to repaint his office the minute Lizzie was out of his life, reverting to the dull off-white he was accustomed to, but he had to admit, she was right. The color she'd picked looked good. She talked too much and spoke her mind and was easily distracted, but she was good at her chosen profession. Very good. Looking at the wall, he couldn't help but remember how he'd watched her paint and sway those hips, how he'd sneaked up behind her and touched her. He never should've done that; he knew it now.

How the hell was he going to get her out of his head?

After a brief knock, the door swung open and one of his most valuable agents, the bony-thin, long-haired, tattooed Curtis Rush breezed in. If Sam hadn't known Curt well, he'd swear the man was a druggie who could not be trusted within ten feet of a working man's wallet.

Curt waved a manila file as he approached Sam's desk. "Got pictures of mama and some guy she just met doin' the nasty on the hood of a car outside a party where drugs weren't only present, they were damn near required. Also have a half-dozen witnesses who will swear she does drugs on a regular basis. She's not particular, from what I hear, but she's developed a fondness for meth." He tossed the folder onto Sam's desk. "Hence the missing teeth." The thin man scowled. "Not only should she not get custody, she shouldn't even have un-supervised visitation rights, and we can prove it."

None of them enjoyed working child custody cases, but they were a necessary evil—and no one was better than Curt when it came to getting people to talk. Sam could walk into a room and there were always some who smelled cop. Curt didn't have that problem.

Curt collapsed bonelessly into Sam's visitor's chair. "I hear you have a girlfriend. About time. When do I get to meet her?"

Great. Word was out. "I don't have a girlfriend."

"Sure you do. The pretty painter with the purple Taser. Marilyn approves, in case you wondered."

"Lizzie's just the daughter of an old friend, that's all."

"Yeah, whatever." Curt stood with a strange, lanky grace. "When do I get to meet her?"

"Since she's currently under twenty-four-hour guard, probably sooner than you'd like."

Sam would be calling on all his employees and a few contract workers to watch Lizzie, because he didn't trust himself to do it.

"Kinky," Curt said with a wink, and then he headed for the door. "The color in here looks nice. What is that, some shade of taupe?"

Chapter 9

Lizzie had never listed speed as one of her attributes as a painter, but today she called on all the speed she could muster. Thank goodness Danny had painted before! They finished the parlor in no time and then moved on to Jenna's room, taking only the shortest break for lunch. She wanted out of this house, but not before she'd made Jenna's room pretty. The time for Jenna to come home from school came and went. The house seemed so empty without the child in it. Lizzie actually found herself fighting tears as she painted. Nothing had worked out as she'd planned. Nothing! No sister, no Sam…

They worked past what would normally be quitting time, so they could finish this room and pack up their supplies. Connelly silently looked in on the workers now and then, but he didn't say a word, not about Jenna, not about anything.

Lizzie knew she wouldn't be back in this house, not ever again. She was contracted to paint a couple more rooms, but the deposit she'd collected would pay for the work she'd done. Being here was more painful than she'd imagined, and she knew damn well Connelly didn't want her here.

Had that been Sam's plan all along? Had he known how this would hurt? Did he think if she hurt badly enough she'd give up? No. She'd insisted that he get her in here, and if he'd told her it wasn't a good idea, she wouldn't have believed him. She'd believe him now. Too late.

She was tempted to grab a hairbrush or toothbrush while she was in Jenna's room, but not only was she pretty sure neither would be sufficient, she couldn't bring herself to steal from the girl. Besides, Jenna would say something about the missing items and Connelly, the bastard, would know. She wouldn't give him the satisfaction. It wasn't like she had any doubts left. Jenna *was* her sister.

Lizzie was headed toward the kitchen and the back door with her hands full when she heard the front door open. She held her breath, wondering if she'd hear Jenna's young voice one more time. Her little sister might've come home to collect something she needed for the night, or else to check out her newly painted room. Instead she heard the shrill voice of Connelly's girlfriend.

"Hey, honey," she called. "I got those brochures from the boarding school today. Come take a look!"

Lizzie stopped dead in her tracks and set down the paint cans she carried. Boarding school?

In the background Connelly hissed, "For God's sake, Heather, keep your voice down!"

"Why? You said the brat would be out of the house tonight."

The brat. Lizzie's heart sank. Her knees went weak. Her hands shook. She stood there, not walking forward, not moving back. She'd been a few steps away from leaving here certain that Jenna was well cared for and loved, and better off not knowing she might have a sister who wanted to be a part of her life. Just a few steps, and she would've been in the backyard, too far away to hear Heather's grating voice talking about boarding schools and brats.

But she couldn't unhear those words—and didn't want to. Wasn't this the very reason she'd come here, pain and all? She needed to know whether or not Jenna was loved and cared for, and now she knew.

Lizzie spun around and walked out of the kitchen and down a short hallway, into the foyer, which was as large as her living room. The two conspirators stood there, heads together, voices lowered.

"Boarding school?" Lizzie asked sharply. "Are you insane?"

Both looked at her, but only Heather's eyes widened. "Darryl, why is the painter talking to us?"

He ignored her. "It's merely an option we're considering."

"An option," Heather said shrilly. "You said when we were married the kid would be out of the house." She looked at Lizzie. "Not that I have anything against kids, mind you, but it's hard to be really romantic when there's a child down the hall, and it messes up our plans so many times. We can't take a long weekend, we can't go anywhere on the spur of the moment. It's a real pain in the ass."

Lizzie looked at Connelly, square on. No more playing games, no more hiding the truth. "I think I might be your stepdaughter's half sister."

He didn't miss a beat as he said, "Harold Aldridge didn't have any other children that I'm aware of."

"You know very well who I am," Lizzie said, stepping toward the man, wishing she had her Taser handy. She really didn't like the way Connelly was looking at her. "You knew when you wrote that check yesterday, or shortly thereafter. Maybe you had to make a few phone calls or check out some things on the Internet, but you know damn well that Charlie Porter is my father, and I suspect you also know that he might be Jenna's father, too."

"I know no such thing," Connelly said. "I suggest you get out of my house, Miss Porter, and don't come back. If I have to call the police…"

"Call them!" she interrupted. "Please."

His eyes went hard. "How much do you want?"

"What?"

"Money," he snapped. "How much money do you want to walk away and leave us in peace?"

"I don't want your money," Lizzie said, horrified and insulted. "I just wanted to make sure that Jenna is all right. I'd almost convinced myself that she was, but now I'm not so sure."

"What are you going to do?" Connelly asked.

"I haven't decided."

He took a menacing step toward her. "The last thing I need is this upset for Jenna, and for myself. I've worked very hard to be a father to a child who has no one else."

"Being a father to a lovely girl shouldn't be so much work," Lizzie argued.

"You have no idea," Connelly muttered. He took another step toward her, and his hand began to rise.

"What's up?" Danny's voice was bright and ignorant. "Are we finished? Do we have everything?"

Connelly took a step away from Lizzie and lowered his hand. Had he really been about to *hit* her? Or had her imagination gotten the best of her? "Miss Porter was just leaving."

Heather had to step into the conversation. "But what was she saying about…" Connelly stopped her with a very firm hand on her arm.

"She's leaving, and she's not coming back. Isn't that right, Miss Porter?"

Lizzie stared at him and answered honestly. "I haven't decided." With that she turned and allowed Danny to escort her out of the house. She was shaking as she reached for the driver's side door handle, and wasn't really surprised when Danny put his hand over hers.

"You want to tell me what happened in there?" he asked kindly.

Unable to speak, Lizzie shook her head.

"I'm driving," Danny said, taking the keys from her hand, "and we're going straight to the office."

"I don't think Sam wants to see me," she said, the words hurting more than they should.

"Too bad," Danny muttered.

Sam usually got an early start and stayed late. His business was his life, and he liked it that way. Agents came and went even on a Friday night, even after Marilyn left for the day at her usual four-thirty.

He wasn't surprised when Danny walked into his office, but he was shocked to see Lizzie right behind him. It wasn't just her presence that surprised him, but the expression on her face. She was more terrified than she'd been last night when bullets had come blazing into her home.

"What's wrong?" he asked, standing and stepping around the desk.

Danny stopped in his tracks, and Lizzie walked around him, headed straight for Sam. "He knows," she said, her voice shaking. "I think he fired Mary Scott because she recommended me, so he didn't know all along but he knows now."

Sam nodded to Danny, and the agent left the room, closing the door behind him.

Lizzie walked straight into Sam's arms, and he couldn't make himself push her away.

"He and that horrible woman are going to get married and send Jenna to a boarding school. Heather called Jenna a brat. A brat! Having a kid in the house cramps her style, and she can't wait to get rid of Jenna. The kid deserves better. I could give her better, if I had the chance. I could take good care of her and be there every night and…and…I would never call her a brat, and I don't have any style to be cramped."

Sam found himself smoothing Lizzie's hair, soothing her the only way he knew how—well, the only way he would allow himself. His mind was spinning as she chattered on. Darryl Connelly. Would Connelly think that shooting at Lizzie would scare her enough to keep her out of his hair? Would he go to such extremes to warn her off, to make sure Jenna never found out she might have a half sister? Last night's bullets had been aimed high, intended to scare, not kill. In theory. Could be the shooter was a lousy shot, and if he'd had a chance to get closer and see inside the house he'd be more efficient.

He tried to be reasonable. It made no sense at all for Connelly to take wild shots at Lizzie. His mind took him there because he was desperate for someone to blame besides himself. "When Jenna is grown you can contact her, and if she's agreeable she can take a blood test and…"

"When she's grown," Lizzie mumbled into his shirt, anger added to her sorrow. "How long will that be? Ten years? Fifteen? Twenty? How many of those years will she spend at boarding school without any family close by? Dad would have a fit if he heard about this. You know he would."

"Lots of kids go to boarding school and like it just fine," he said, trying to be practical.

"Do they?" she asked, now angry enough to pull away from him and look up with teary, warm eyes. "Kids actually *like* being shuffled off to a dorm somewhere?"

He knew lots of kids who would be better off in such a situation, but he didn't say so. Not now. That wouldn't help matters at all. Time to get tough. "The truth of the matter is, you have no legal rights where Jenna is concerned. You may or may not be a half sister."

"She looks just like Charlie!"

"She shares a few relatively common characteristics. That's not proof."

"There could be a blood test. Damn, I should've grabbed that toothbrush after all. We could get a judge to order…"

"Good luck getting that to happen," Sam said sourly. Connelly had enough money to hire an army of lawyers who could block such a request for years.

Lizzie pursed her lips for a moment. Her eyes narrowed. "Okay, hotshot P.I., explain this to me. Yesterday Darryl Connelly finds out my last name is Porter. Today he knows why I'm there. He didn't say so, but I could see and hear it. Mrs. Scott is gone, and I'll bet if you talk to her she'll tell you she was fired. I don't believe for a minute that she quit. Connelly gets Jenna out of the house so I can't see her even one more time, and then he makes a point of telling me how much he loves and cares for her—before I find out he wants to send her away, that is. The only way he could've figured out who I am so quickly is if he already knew that Jenna's real father's name is Porter. He probably did a little checking on the Internet. Charlie's obit names me as his daughter, so it's not exactly a stretch. I'm thinking Jenna's mother told Connelly the truth somewhere along the way, and now he's scared that I'm going to stir the pot."

There were a lot of suppositions there, but her theories were sound.

"I'll check into it."

Lizzie was too close; she leaned into him slightly, warm and soft and splattered with dried paint. His body responded to hers, much as it had last night. The difference was, he realized now that he was the worst man in the world for her.

"Will you come home with me?" she asked simply. "I'll cook you supper, and maybe we can pick up where we left off last night."

He didn't hesitate to respond. "I can't."

"Can't come to the house or can't pick up where we left off?"

"Can't do either."

She didn't move away. "I was afraid you felt that

way, but I had to be sure. It's very sad. I mean, I never really had you, not even last night when we were so close and it seemed like everything was about to change, but it feels like I've lost something important. I miss you," she said simply. "You're standing right here, touching me, and I *miss* you."

"You won't be alone," he said, trying to ignore the depth of her confession. "Someone will be watching the house. If there's any sign of trouble, all you have to do is call."

"But not you, I'm guessing," she said softly. "I won't be calling *you*."

"No."

She backed away slowly, all but peeling her body from his. Already he missed her weight against him, the smell of paint and woman.

"Too bad. It could've been great, even if it wasn't meant to last."

If Lizzie was one of those women who were given to begging for what she wanted, he might be in for a tough fight, but that wasn't in her nature. There was a sadness in her eyes and a reluctant biting of her lips, but she would not plead or cry to get what she wanted. She'd made herself available and he'd turned her down. That would be the end of it.

She turned and walked away, and suddenly he felt as she did, as if he'd lost something special. Something he'd never truly had.

In the mood for carbs and lots of them, Lizzie made spaghetti for supper. Besides, she needed to keep busy, and her usual microwave meal or can of soup would be done too soon. Her mind whirled as she cooked. She didn't have Sam. Never had. Mourning the loss of something which had never been hers was pointless.

So she thought about Jenna. It shouldn't be too terribly difficult to find out where Jenna was going to be sent to school. In August or September, the girl would be packed up and moved there, leaving her beautiful blue room behind.

Lizzie would be right behind her. She'd sell the house and start her business all over again, no matter where that might be. There were always people who wanted their homes freshened up. It might take her some time to build the business up again, but with the money from the sale of the house she'd be fine, for a while. She could find a way to meet Jenna, maybe give the school a great discount on her painting services and manage to "accidentally" bump into Jenna and strike up a conversation.

Where she'd go from there she didn't know, but Jenna would have a friend when she was sent away to boarding school. She would *not* be alone.

Maybe it was a little sad that her entire life was built around the sister—yes, sister, not half sister, not maybe-sister, but *sister*—she barely knew, but she'd work with what she'd been given.

Besides, at the moment getting out of Birmingham sounded like a very good idea.

Showered and dressed in yoga pants and a long T-shirt, she went onto the front porch and motioned to her guard for the evening—muscular, blond, oft-broken-nosed Mike—to come inside. She had made enough spaghetti to feed a small army, since it was impossible to make spaghetti for one, and she might as well feed her bodyguard. Besides, if he stayed out there in his car all night, the neighbors would talk.

Mike was sheepish about coming inside, but he liked spaghetti. She wasn't much of a cook, but she could handle spaghetti, as long as the sauce came out of a jar. It was nice to cook for someone who ate well and appreciated the chef's efforts. Lizzie ate much less, and she did most of the talking through dinner—choosing innocuous subjects like the weather and favorite television shows—and even though she didn't know Mike at all beyond the quick introductions that had been made at Sam's office, she liked him well enough, and tonight she needed the company.

Lizzie wished, for a moment, that she could be one of those carefree girls who just went from one man to the next as it suited her. Love was not required. Any man—unattached and healthy, of course—would do. Maybe she'd keep a man for a day or a week or a month before someone better caught her eye, but at least she wouldn't be forever alone.

Mike was handsome and strong. Manly, if not terribly bright. Did he have a girlfriend? Lizzie's stomach got heavy, and it wasn't the spaghetti. She'd be just like her mother if she took that route. She didn't want to be the kind of woman who would break a good man's heart in the name of her own pleasure and comfort, the way a flighty wife had broken Charlie's heart.

Maybe one day the right man would come along, but at the moment the right man was being terribly stubborn.

Lizzie jumped when the phone rang, but when she checked the caller ID and saw her neighbor's name there, she relaxed and sighed. Garet Miles was middle-aged and odd, and like Lizzie, he lived alone.

"Hello."

"Lizzie, hi," Garet said brightly. "I just wanted to make sure everything was okay. Your place is usually so quiet, but last night I saw a strange car in the driveway, then there were what sounded like gunshots, and then there were police cars and lights very late, and now there's yet another strange car in the driveway. What gives?"

She hated to lie, but the truth was impossible. *I'm under twenty-four-hour guard* was not what the neighbors wanted to hear. "I had a date last night, and then some kids driving by shot into the living room, which is why the police came by, and tonight I'm having a friend over for dinner."

"A friend," he said, cooler than before. "Have you started dating again?"

Bypass the shooting and the police and go straight to the dating thing. Lizzie tried not to sigh into the phone. He'd hear her if she gave in to her instinctive response. Garet was a dozen years older than she and what anyone would call an odd bird. He'd asked her out right after she'd moved in, and she'd told him she wasn't ready to date. It hadn't been a lie, exactly. She still wasn't ready to date *him* and never would be.

Funny. Sam was eight years older, but those years didn't seem to matter. They had a lot of problems, but age wasn't one of them. With Garet, the twelve-year difference seemed like aeons.

"Not really," she said. "Tonight certainly isn't a date, and last night was an exception for an old friend I hadn't seen in many years." That wasn't entirely a lie.

"Oh." That single word held a world of disappointment.

"I have to go." Lizzie tried to sound cheerful, but as she hung up she realized that weird neighbors were yet another reason for her to sell this house and move away.

* * *

Long after dark Sam drove by Lizzie's house, knowing it was wrong but unable to stay away. He couldn't sleep if he didn't know she was safe. Everything was quiet up and down the street. The only sign that things were not right was the boarded-up window—and the empty car sitting in her driveway behind her pickup.

The first time he drove by and saw that Mike wasn't in his car, he assumed that the diligent bodyguard, who could usually scare away unwanted visitors with a glare and a flexing of impressive muscles, was walking around the yard, checking the perimeter, doing his job and then some. The second time, he realized it was more likely that Mike was inside the house—and had been for at least two hours.

He picked up his cell to call Mike, but before he could pull up the man's cell number, the phone rang.

He said a very bad word when he saw the name on the caller ID. His ex-wife had started calling now and then. Since her latest divorce just six months ago, she'd asked him to look at her rattling car, fix the garbage disposal, change a lightbulb she couldn't reach and mow her backyard. He'd listened to the car and checked the garbage disposal, but when she'd made it clear those weren't the only husbandly duties she wanted him to perform, he quit going over there. That was a trap he did not intend to fall into again. He'd started keeping a list of competent handymen around and was always happy to share their phone numbers with her.

"Dottie Ann," he said, answering without the courtesy of a hello. "What do you want?"

She screamed into the phone. "Get your ass over here! Someone took a shot at my house!" And then she started to sob.

Chapter 10

The squad car pulled up to Dottie Ann's neat ranch at almost exactly the same time Sam did. Thank God he wouldn't have to face her alone. He wouldn't have come at all, if this wasn't two nights in a row that someone had taken a shot at a woman who had the misfortune to be in his life—or in his past.

His ex-wife met him at the door. "You didn't have to call the cops," she said bitterly, ignoring the two uniformed officers behind him.

"Yes, I did. You'll need the police report for the insurance company."

"Oh." She looked as though she wanted to close the door in the officers' faces, but she didn't. The two patrolmen followed Sam into the house.

The scene was clear enough, and all too familiar. The front window was broken, and a single bullet was embedded high in the living room wall.

"Someone shot at me," Dottie Ann said shrilly.

"Were you here when it happened?" Sam asked.

"In the kitchen," she said, her voice trembling slightly.

"See the car?"

"No!" Dottie Ann ran her hands up and down her thin arms, as if trying to warm herself. In another lifetime he would've hugged her and warmed her up himself, but that day was long gone. "I was in the *kitchen,* and I didn't see anything."

Sam sat back while his ex sullenly gave the police officers a brief, almost grudging statement. Sam's mind was spinning. As he'd initially suspected, last night's excitement at Lizzie's led right back to him. Who would do this? Tracking down Dottie Ann, with her new last name and new address, had to have taken some time and research. Not a lot, but the shooting hadn't been random. He'd have to call his family tonight and warn them, though he couldn't be sure the shooter would leave town just to fire a high shot into a relative's house. Still, wouldn't hurt to be safe. It was impossible to tell when a situation like this one would escalate.

The officers promised to follow up with a thorough investigation, and at hearing that, Dottie Ann scoffed. The younger of the two cops blushed, and his lips tightened. Still, he said nothing. Sam remembered too well the crap he'd too often had to take, just for doing his job.

The officers left, and Dottie Ann turned to Sam with pleading eyes. He knew this look.

He stood. "I gotta get out of here and make some phone calls."

"You're leaving me alone?" she all but screeched.

"Yeah." Sam's voice remained even, steady. "Don't

worry. Someone's already on their way to board up the window until it can be replaced." He'd made that call from the car. Tonight he wasn't sticking around to help.

Dottie Ann's eyes hardened. Her face was so unyielding and sour Sam wondered how he'd ever thought she was beautiful. She was one of those women who looked gorgeous on first sight, but the more time spent with her the more her beauty began to fade.

"You're going back to her, aren't you?" his ex snapped. "You're running out of here leaving me all alone so you can hook up with that…that mousy kid."

How the hell had Dottie Ann found out about Lizzie? "I'm going home."

"I seriously doubt that. Does she still have a crush on you? Does she still moon after you and sigh when you so much as look in her direction? That's sick. I'll bet she does everything you tell her to do, and I bet you like it. Having a girl like that one around has to be good for a man's ego."

"You don't have any idea what you're talking about."

"Someone shot at me, and you can't get out of here fast enough! I can't stay here alone! You can't leave me!" There was sad desperation in her voice, a fire in her eyes.

"Call a friend, go to a hotel, move," Sam said coldly as he moved toward the front door and opened it, anxious to escape. "Trust me, if someone wanted you dead, you'd be dead."

Dottie Ann's apprehension passed quickly, and Sam saw the unkind woman he had come to know too well. "Yeah, you'd know about that, wouldn't you?" she snapped, standing in the open doorway, her voice rising as Sam walked to his car, which was parked by the curb. The officers hadn't left; they stood by the front of the patrol car, examining their paperwork by the light of a bright flashlight. Making sure all the *i*'s were dotted and the *t*'s crossed, he imagined. "At least I know it wasn't you, even though you so obviously hate me!" Dottie Ann called shrilly. "If you took a shot at me I'd be dead enough, shot right between the eyes. Isn't that how you do it? Isn't that the way it works, Sam?" With that, she slammed the front door.

The cops were no longer looking at their paperwork. They both stared at Sam, and he felt the world start to spin a little. Every time he thought this was behind him, some asshole brought it up again. Strangely enough, that asshole was usually his ex. The younger of the two officers headed his way, and Sam wondered what kind of interrogation he was in for. Sure enough, the kid asked.

"That was you? You're Sam Travers?"

"Yeah," Sam said, not bothering to lie or hide or cower. That wasn't his way. No matter what the kid had to say, he'd endure it. It wouldn't be anything he hadn't heard before. Trigger-happy. Baby killer. Gunslinger. Rogue. Even Lizzie had gotten in on the deal. What had she said when he'd drawn his gun on Skinner? Overkill.

The young officer smiled and offered his hand. "Hot damn, I sure would like to shake your hand."

Sam was so taken aback he didn't immediately take the proffered hand. Eventually he did, for a brief hand-shake. The kid seemed genuine enough, but hell, no one wanted to be congratulated for taking a life, even if it had happened years ago. What was this kid, a hot gun with an itchy trigger finger? Did he think they were two of a kind?

"Seth Talbot is my older brother," the kid said, and

suddenly the congratulations made some sense. "He said he'd be dead if not for you."

"How is he?" Sam asked, remembering the officer who'd been bleeding on the ground, in and out of consciousness on that night. He'd never seen so much blood, and had been certain if Talbot wasn't DOA, he sure as hell wouldn't make it through the night. One cop had been dead on the scene that night, and when Sam had first arrived he'd thought it was going to be even worse.

"He's had lots of therapy," the younger Talbot said, "but he's doing really great. Got married, had a little girl, went back to school… His life is good." His expression hardened. "I know you took a lot of crap, but some of us know Seth wouldn't be here today if not for you. Same for the other fella that was injured."

For the first time in a long time, Sam admitted the truth out loud. He told this kid the reality that ate at him every day. "If I had to do it all over again, I wouldn't change a thing." Not even knowing that it would cost him his job, his wife, his faith in people as a whole. What he'd done was *right,* and he wasn't going to apologize anymore.

"Right on, brother," Talbot said, and then he looked toward the house. "You used to be married to her?"

"Yep."

"So sorry, man," Talbot said sincerely. "So *very* sorry."

Sam got into his car and drove off, feeling as if he were making a hasty escape. He made phone calls as he drove, trying to warn his family of potential danger without alarming them. He doubted anyone would go all the way to Arizona to harass his sister, but Atlanta and his brother were just a couple of hours away, and

Sarasota was less than a day's drive. The calls were quick and a little unpleasant—especially where his mother was concerned. She was always harping on him to go back to school and get a safe job. Soon enough that task was taken care of, and before Sam realized what he was doing, where he was going, he found himself on Lizzie's street.

Lizzie laughed, sitting on the couch with her feet tucked beneath her. Mike, looking comfy on the other end of the long couch, wasn't as dumb as he appeared at first glance. There was a brain behind that bent nose that looked perfectly at home on a square boxer's face. A fighter boxer, not a dog boxer. He was actually pretty funny, too. They'd eaten, watched some television and eventually found a basketball game to watch halfheartedly.

Lizzie hadn't even looked toward the television since Mike started telling her about some of his more interesting cases. Never a dull moment!

Apparently Mike was still on the job. In spite of the noise from the television and her laughter, his head snapped up when a car slowed down in front of her house. They heard the change in the engine, the low rumble. They couldn't see anything, because she still had plywood in place of a front window. Mike rose from the couch with surprising grace for such a big guy, and he gripped Lizzie's arm with meaty fingers, guiding her toward the stairs. "Go," he ordered in a gruff voice.

"It's probably…" Before she could say *nothing,* Mike glared at her and drew the gun he'd had tucked at his spine. Lizzie grudgingly climbed the stairs, muttering to herself. "This would *not* be a good time to be a door-to-door salesman in this neighborhood."

Instead of continuing on to her bedroom, Lizzie stopped at the top of the stairs and listened as Mike opened the front door.

"You're supposed to be watching the house, not moving in."

Lizzie instinctively relaxed when she heard Sam's voice. She leaned into the wall and strained to hear every word. It wasn't difficult; they weren't so very far away.

"I'm supposed to watch Lizzie, and that's what I'm doing," Mike argued calmly. "If you don't like the way I'm handling this assignment, then give me more specific instructions."

Sam stepped into the house and the door was closed behind him. Lizzie tried not to breathe too hard. If he moved this way, he could very easily glance up the stairs and see her. If he headed toward the couch, she'd remain hidden. She wanted to hear him speak when he didn't know she was listening. He was always so on guard around her.

"Someone just fired a shot into my ex's front window," Sam said harshly.

"Anyone hurt?" Mike didn't sound overly concerned. Maybe he'd met Dottie Ann.

"No."

"Will we be watching her house 24/7, too, until we know what's up?"

Sam sighed. He mumbled a curse word. "I suppose we should. Head over that way and drive by. Park down the street and keep an eye on things. The carpenter should be there boarding up the window, and she might have called a friend. If she's not by herself or if she hightails it out of there, you can head home. If she is alone, you can go in and sit with her, if you want to."

Mike gave a harsh, short bark of laughter. "No, thanks, boss. I'd rather sit in my car. What about Lizzie?"

Again, a hesitation. "I'm staying," Sam said, his voice low and hard.

Lizzie's heart fluttered; her mouth went dry, the way it did when Sam was near. So, he was staying. Here. Would he sit outside in his car, awake all night and watching her house? She really couldn't see them sitting on the couch and laughing the way she had with Mike. She couldn't even see them getting physically close— as in, in the same room for more than five minutes— without matters quickly spiraling out of control.

Mike called out a thanks and left, and the house was instantly too quiet. Lizzie didn't move; she didn't rush down the steps with a smile plastered on her face. She stood at the top of the stairs, leaning against the wall, waiting. Good heavens, she had no idea what would happen next.

Sam moved almost silently to the bottom of the staircase. He looked up, not at all surprised to see her standing there. "Someone shot at my ex."

"I heard."

"As I suspected, this is all on me."

"Good to know no one's out to get me because they think I painted their walls pink." Lizzie tried to smile, but Sam wasn't smiling and her attempt was sad and short-lived.

He placed a foot on the bottom step. "All I could think about as I was standing there listening to my ex rail was you." He did not sound happy about the remembrance. "I couldn't get out of there fast enough."

"Well…" Lizzie began, totally understanding that. He didn't let her say anything more.

"This is a bad idea." He took a step up, and then another. "I'm not the right man for you. Hell, I'm not the right man for any decent woman."

"Maybe I'm not all *that* decent," Lizzie said, her voice higher and slightly more panicked than she'd like it to be. Her heart pounded so hard she was certain he must be able to hear it. He was steady. Why couldn't she be?

"You're the most decent person I've ever known," he said.

"Not…"

"Which is why if you tell me to get lost now, I will. I'll sit in my car and watch the house until relief arrives in the morning, and then I'll get out of your life for good." He stopped, halfway up the staircase. Close, but not nearly close enough.

She swallowed hard. The idea of life without Sam in it was simply wrong. It hurt, in a way she had not expected. He wasn't hers; he had never been hers. She didn't kid herself that he was making her any kind of lifelong promise. He wanted her tonight. They might never have anything more.

And even though it went against everything she believed about the way a relationship between a man and a woman *should* be, she wanted whatever she could have from Sam. One night, two, maybe a dozen, if she was lucky.

"Don't stop," she said.

He continued up the stairs, each step solid and deliberate. When he was almost to her, Lizzie found she was holding her breath. Her heart continued to pound. "Are you on the pill?" he asked. "The patch, whatever it is women are using these days?"

"Yes," Lizzie answered.

"Good." Sam was right in front of her now, his blue eyes boring into her, his hands warm and heavy on her waist. She was trapped between the wall at her back and a wall of Sam, and it was nice. No, not nice; having him so close was powerful and exhilarating and tempting beyond belief. It was as if she could already feel him touching her, kissing her.

"I didn't think you would come back," she whispered.

"Neither did I," he said, his voice almost as soft as hers.

"I didn't think—"

He interrupted her, moving his mouth toward hers. "Don't speak, Lizzie. Don't think." And then he kissed her, and it was very easy to stop thinking, to just follow where her body—and his—led.

They kissed, this meeting of mouths hungry and touched with desperation. Not a bad desperation, but still—desperate. She would have taken a step toward the bedroom, that was only logical, but she was pinned against the wall, lost in heat and longing and desire that rippled through her body and kept her all but glued to Sam. He lowered his lips to her throat, and she took the opportunity to take a deep breath that burned her lungs. Everything in her burned. Every fiber, every cell. When Sam moved his hands to the waistband of her yoga pants she had to wonder… "Here?" And then she remembered his instruction. *Don't think. Don't think.*

So she didn't think as he shimmied her pants and panties down; she just stepped out of them when they were around her ankles.

It was good not to think, she decided as he aroused her with gentle fingers, as he kissed her and stroked where she was on fire. It was fine not to think as she reached out and unfastened his belt and unzipped his trousers, almost but not quite frantically reaching for him, freeing him and guiding him toward her. He was hard, long, incredibly hot. A rough gasp of a plea rumbled in her throat. She was empty without him; she burned and ached and yearned. She'd never needed anyone or anything this way. His fingers stroked; she shifted her body, trying to bring him closer.

Sam lifted her, pressed her body against the wall, and finally—finally!—guided the head of his penis into her. There was relief at the gently stretching entry of his body into her, relief and a renewed drive all rolled into one. She wanted him to plunge deep; she wanted all of him, now, but he teased her, moving slowly, giving her some of what she needed but not all. He rocked gently; he eased into her. For a long while Lizzie held her breath, waiting and wanting. Her body trembled; when she breathed again her breath came hard. When she couldn't bear it anymore she took control, as best she could, shifting her hips and lowering herself with a sway and a dip, lowering herself down to take him deep.

As soon as he touched her deeply, release washed through her body, hard and amazing. She made a noise that was somewhere between a groan and a moan and a cry of joy as her inner muscles spasmed and danced. It was a good thing Sam held her, because otherwise she would fall to the floor, a boneless puddle of happiness and perfect contentment and complete exhaustion. He was still hard inside her, still moving ever so slightly. She laughed and kissed his neck, tasted his sweat, held on as if for dear life.

"I'm beginning to think we'll never get entirely naked and into my bed." She was breathless and satisfied and happier than she'd been in a very long time.

Sam nudged her, then trailed his mouth along her throat, moving slowly until he came to her ear, where he whispered, "Wanna bet?"

Chapter 11

Completely naked and in Lizzie's bed at last, Sam picked up where they'd left off in the hallway. Sliding into her wet heat, losing himself in her in more ways than one. He hadn't planned to take her against the wall, not for their first time, but once he'd had her in his arms he'd discovered he couldn't bear to let her go. She wasn't the only one who'd stopped thinking.

Beneath him she was warm and soft and willing, lost in passion and seemingly surprised by the depth of her response and her need for more. In a very Lizzie way she was completely open and honest about what she wanted. She didn't play games, didn't jockey for position or try to find the power play in something as simple and powerful as sex. Already she was moving against him as if on the verge of another orgasm, so soon after the last.

He'd wanted to get lost in someone or something tonight. Driving down the road, burned by the past and worried about the future and angry at the world—the way he'd been for such a long time—all he could think of was Lizzie. Only she would wipe away the hurt and the memories he tried so hard to bury deep. Only the sight of her smile and the feel of her body against his would make the world right again. She thought she needed him; he needed her more.

Lizzie wrapped her legs around him, higher, tighter, and clasped his hips in trembling hands. She sighed, in pleasure and need, and once again Sam silenced the annoying thoughts in his head and experienced nothing beyond physical need and drive.

She came again, clasping her body to his, gasping, searching, and as she did, he let himself go. Release ripped through him and together he and Lizzie grappled on the bed as the last waves of their shared response flitted through their bodies and left them spent.

"Amazing," Lizzie said breathlessly, her hands resting on his arms, her legs still wrapped around his. There was little illumination in the room—only a hint from the streetlight through the window and a touch of hallway light to see Lizzie by—but he could see enough to realize that she was beautiful and mussed and satisfied and, yes, amazed.

He felt guilty for needing her tonight, for realizing that no one else would do, for taking her when he knew he couldn't be the man she wanted or needed. But he didn't feel guilty enough to apologize and scurry out of her bed and her life. Maybe he wasn't everything she deserved, but he would make their time together worthwhile. She wouldn't regret tonight, or any night to come.

"Amazing is right," he said, lowering his head to kiss her throat. Lizzie was all but melting into the mattress.

"I've never—" she took a deep breath "—well, not never exactly, but not like *that* and not twice. And not for a very long time. Really, the difference is like comparing a small scoop of fat-free vanilla ice cream to a banana split with all the fixings. Except nuts. I don't like nuts. Oh, except yours, of course." She bit her lower lip. "I've said too much, haven't I?"

"Never," Sam whispered. A new thought nagged at him as he reluctantly rolled away from Lizzie. "If there's no boyfriend, no recent servings of fat-free vanilla ice cream, then why are you on birth control?" A horrid thought struck him. She'd lied. She'd decided to create the family she so desperately desired by having a child of her own, and she'd told him what he wanted to hear. The thought didn't last long. Lizzie didn't lie, and her soft giggle told him that wasn't the case this time around.

"I'm horribly optimistic," she said, her voice not quite as breathless as before. "And I *do* like to plan ahead."

"Prep work."

"Exactly," she responded.

They lay side by side in her bed for a while, lost in silent companionship. Sam's earlier demons had faded; they never entirely went away. He was as content and comfortable as he could remember being in…years. Now and then Lizzie reached out to touch him, her fingers gentle and arousing but not grasping or purposely seductive.

She placed the tip of a finger on his cheek. "Where did you get this scar? I've been dying to ask."

"Bar fight," he said simply.

"Really? You don't strike me as the bar fight kinda guy."

He didn't want to tell her that he'd been falling down drunk at the time, that the fight had been about the shooting. So instead he responded, a hint of teasing in his voice, "You should've seen the other guy."

She didn't pursue the matter, but kissed his cheek and settled comfortably against him in silence.

After a while she said, "Do you know what I want?"

Sadly, he was afraid he did know. "Nope," he responded.

"I've never made love in the shower before, or in the bathtub. Which is best?" she asked, her voice quick. "Do you have a preference? Not that I'd want you to do anything you don't want to. For all I know you have a fear of water. I love the water, and it seems like it would be the perfect combination, you and the shower, or you and the bath. I do need to get cleaned up, that's for sure, and...though, sorry, I don't guess that's very romantic. Not that this is at all romantic," she said, her voice rising slightly. "It's just sex, I know that, I really do. People do it all the—"

Sam silenced her the best way he knew how. He rolled over and kissed her, taking her mouth with his just as she was about to say *time*. When she was completely relaxed and into the kiss, he gently drew away. "Both," he whispered.

"Both what?" she asked.

Sam smiled. The kiss had made her forget; she was so easily distractible. "Not bath *or* shower, bath *and* shower. After all, we have all night, don't we?"

"And I don't have any plans for tomorrow," she offered, wrapping her arms around his neck.

"Neither do I." At least, nothing that couldn't be changed with a phone call.

They slept, but not much. Lizzie was surprised to find that she literally couldn't get enough of Sam. She was also surprised by her own response, finding fulfillment again and again, demanding more and more even though her body was slightly sore and her mind was fogged with lack of sleep.

She was so fogged—and loopy—she almost told Sam that she loved him, more than once. She knew why he was here, and love had nothing to do with it. This was sex. Sex as she had never imagined it could be, but still, sex. He wouldn't want to hear her talk about love. The word would probably scare him away, and she didn't want that. She'd have to convince him she was satisfied with the sex. And she *was* satisfied, amazingly so.

Not too long after dawn, Sam led her to the upstairs bath at the end of the hall and the oversize tub; they'd showered there the night before. Lizzie found herself laughing, demanding, teasing…and then completely lost in Sam's body and her own. She would never be able to take a bath here again without thinking of the splash of water on her skin and Sam's, the way she straddled him to ease the pain of the wanting that never seemed to fade, the way he came inside her. The way she'd almost uttered the words he didn't want to hear. After they stumbled back to the bed, Sam grabbed his cell and made a phone call. He canceled someone's shift as her bodyguard, and Lizzie smiled as she drifted toward a deep sleep. He wasn't leaving. Not yet.

She woke a while later to find Sam's hands on her as he urged her closer. Lizzie laughed a little. "I love this, I cannot get enough of you, but to be honest, I'm a little sore."

His face turned deadly serious. "Really?"

"Really. I'm sore all over. Thighs, arms, my right shoulder…" What position had irritated her shoulder? Apparently, she wasn't quite as flexible as she'd thought she was. "I hurt everywhere." She didn't bother to continue elaborating, nor did she explain that she'd never before spent an entire night making love, that she'd never before come again and again.

Sam was relentless. He didn't move away and leave her alone. "Everywhere?"

"Everywhere."

He rose up slightly to look at her with those amazingly expressive blue eyes. "Kiss it and make it better?"

Without waiting for an answer, he did just that. Her shoulder, her arms, her thighs, he kissed every sore muscle—and then some. He "made it better" until she was lost in a haze of amazing sensation, until she screamed and her body arched off the mattress.

Lizzie fell into another dreamless, exhausted, completely satisfied sleep. She woke to what looked to be midafternoon light coming into her bedroom. The ache had not subsided, but it was a gentle, warm, completely acceptable ache. She was happier than she had ever been.

Until she looked at the other side of the bed and realized that Sam wasn't there.

She'd never fooled herself into thinking that Sam was something he wasn't. He wasn't a man who stayed; he wasn't a man who stuck around after the fun was over. He wasn't going to bring her breakfast in bed and tell her she was the most wonderful woman he'd ever known and while she ate omelets and cinnamon rolls tell her that he loved her and always had. He wasn't going to get down on one knee and propose to her, deciding after one night of passion that he couldn't live without her. No, that wasn't who he was, and she knew it too well. He'd told her right off the bat that he liked being single and that wasn't going to change. Still, she'd expected he'd wait around until she was awake. Was that too much to ask?

She glanced around the room, which looked as if a tornado had come through in the night. Her bedcovers were on the other side of the room, and the decorative pillows had been tossed about haphazardly. All that remained on the bed were the bottom sheet, a pillow, and a hopelessly twisted top sheet. Curious as to what time it was, she looked at the bedside table where her clock should be. It wasn't there, but was on the floor near the bedcovers, electrical cord trailing out behind it. They had all but destroyed the room…it had been a night to remember…and Sam had just up and *left?*

Her melancholy mood brightened a bit when she heard what sounded like the clink of a pot drifting up from her kitchen. It was a distant, gentle sound, but it was real. She wouldn't get her hopes up too much, but maybe Sam was a man who made breakfast, after all.

Sam heard Lizzie's soft step on the stairs as he poured the beaten eggs into the pan. Scrambled eggs, bacon cooked in the microwave and toast. That was about as fancy as his cooking got. He turned his head as Lizzie entered her kitchen, wearing a pale blue robe that was too big for her, her hair mussed but slightly tamed, probably with her fingers, her face flushed, her eyes bright.

"You're cooking," she said, as if he'd sprouted another head.

"I do cook, on occasion," he said. "That occasion is usually hunger." And man, he was starving. Last night had sapped him, taken every ounce of his energy. He needed the calories—he needed to sleep for twelve hours or so.

Strangely enough, he could easily skip both food and sleep to be inside Lizzie one more time. On the table, maybe. Was she wearing anything under that robe? He shook off that thought and turned his attention to the eggs. She looked as beat as he did. She needed nourishment, too.

Lizzie shuffled to the stove and looked around him, as the microwave ended its run with a ping. "Were you going to bring me breakfast in bed?"

"Nope," Sam said, taking the skillet off the heat and dumping the eggs onto a large plate. "I was going to yell up the stairs that breakfast was ready and if you didn't hurry down I was going to eat it all myself."

"It's almost three in the afternoon!" she said, obviously shocked as she glanced at the clock on the microwave. "No wonder I'm starving. I tried to check the time on my alarm clock, but somehow it ended up on the floor and unplugged."

"You kicked it off the nightstand."

"I did? Hmm. I don't remember that." She walked toward the full coffeepot, grabbed a mug, reached for the decanter. "Is anyone out front?" she asked as she poured. "I vaguely recall hearing you call someone and cancel a shift, but surely it's time for the next. If there's someone out there, he might want a bite to eat, too."

"An off-duty cop from Tuscaloosa is taking the three to eleven shift," Sam said. "Don't worry. He's not hungry."

Together they managed to smoothly set the table and fill it with food and steaming coffee. It was comfortable—a little bit too comfortable. They ate in silence for a couple of minutes, and then Lizzie slowed her pace and looked at him.

"You didn't say much last night."

He looked her in the eye. "I didn't think you wanted me to *talk*."

"Very funny," she said, smiling. The smile didn't last. "I heard you telling Mike about the shooting at your ex's house. What does that mean?"

"It means someone is out to rile me." He wished she hadn't brought it up; until she'd brought reality crashing down around him he'd been quite happy to stay lost in the unreal world they'd created here—a world that wouldn't last. "You don't need to worry about it."

"Let me guess, you're going to do enough worrying for both of us."

"Yep."

She wagged a piece of crisp bacon at him. "How am I supposed to do what needs to be done if I always have an armed man at my side? Talk about putting a crimp in my style…"

"Think of it this way. You'll have a full-time painter's assistant until the situation is cleared up."

"It's not the painting I'm worried about," she said, stopping to take a bite of the bacon she'd been shaking at him.

"Then what?"

She chewed her bacon, set what remained on her plate, took a sip of coffee and then looked him in the eye. "What about Jenna?"

Sam's stomach tightened. "What are you talking

about? That's done, right? You decided to back off, for now."

Lizzie sighed. "No, it's not done. It was done until I heard that her moron stepfather is planning to send her to boarding school."

"You're not going to tell her about your suspicions."

"You make it sound like I just picked a random child and decided to claim her. Suspicions," she scoffed. "No, I'm not going to tell her." She wrinkled her nose as if she still wasn't a fan of the plan to keep the secret a secret. "But I think she could use a friend."

"Twelve-year-old friends," Sam said, trying not to clench his teeth. "Not fully grown women friends." This could go wrong in so many ways, and in most of the scenarios it was Lizzie who got hurt.

"Have you talked to Mary Scott?"

"Yes," he said, wishing she wouldn't go there.

"Was she fired?"

"Connelly accused her of taking some money he'd left on the desk in his office. She insisted she didn't take it, but he refused to listen to her."

"You know he fired her because she's the one who got me into the house." Lizzie shook her head. "It's so unfair."

"I'll make sure Mrs. Scott gets another, better-paying job. I've already started looking. She's a nice person, really. I don't think she likes Connelly much, and I'm sure she has good reason. Otherwise, she wouldn't have taken the bribe to get us in the house. She'll be fine, I promise."

"Sam Travers, the man who can fix everything."

"Not everything, I'm afraid."

Lizzie looked him squarely in the eye and he was reminded of last night, the way she'd looked at him while he was inside her, the way she'd laughed and touched and given and taken. This was a woman who held nothing back. Not in bed. Not in her life. "Jenna needs me."

Lizzie wasn't surprised when Sam dressed and left the house, not long after their delayed breakfast and semiargument. He remained slightly annoyed that she hadn't given up on being a part of Jenna's life, and communicated that displeasure through pursed lips and hard eyes. She wasn't surprised that whatever man Sam had left on duty—the Tuscaloosa cop—didn't come to the door. He'd probably been ordered to keep his distance. She wasn't surprised when her nosy neighbor Garet called to ask—again—what was going on at her place.

She *was* extremely surprised when, just a few hours after he'd left, Sam returned. He'd showered and changed clothes, and he came bearing shrimp and broccoli, fried rice and sweet and sour chicken, all from her favorite Chinese take-out place.

She didn't even try to deny that she was starving again.

They ate and talked, steering clear of explosive subjects like Jenna and Dottie Ann. The way he looked at her was more than explosive enough. His eyes met hers and she felt it to her bones. *Very* nice. It didn't take her long to realize that he wasn't going to leave her, not tonight. When most of the food was gone he asked her if she had room for dessert. She just smiled and told him a banana split would be nice.

Sam seemed right at home in her little house. She liked it, having him here, having *him,* and she was going to make the best of it while she could. She wasn't foolish enough to think she'd have him in her life for very long, not in the way she wanted.

The way he looked at her when she asked for a banana split…it was a good thing most of her soreness had passed. Hooray for acetaminophen and hot baths and long naps.

He took her in his arms, and she melted there, perfectly content, wonderfully turned-on. Happy. She was so very happy. Could she settle for what Sam had to give her, which was very nice but not at all *everything?*

For tonight, yes. Yes, she could.

Chapter 12

"Now that you're living with Lizzie, do you still want a 24/7 watch?" Danny asked the casual-sounding question as he and Sam covered the too-slim file on the case, rejecting suspects who had unshakable alibis and coming up with new ones to take their places. Someone had shot into Lizzie's house—and into Dottie Ann's—and he wouldn't rest until he knew who. And why.

"I'm not living with Lizzie," Sam said coolly. Maybe he'd been there more often than not in the past several days, maybe he'd been there every night, but he certainly hadn't moved in. Moving in with a woman was a sign of commitment, a big step, a momentous leap forward. He had *not* moved in with Lizzie—though he had managed to leave a toothbrush and a change of clothes there....

"Whatever you call it, a night shift at this point seems

like an unnecessary expense." And unspoken—no one liked to spend all night sitting on the street or in the driveway trying to stay awake while they missed their own wives and girlfriends.

But removing the night shift would mean that Sam would be obligated to stay at Lizzie's all night, and he wasn't there yet. Right now they were taking it one day at a time. They went out to eat, and had seen a movie. She cooked for him; he cooked for her. He stayed with Lizzie because he wanted to, and because she wanted him there. The sex was great, they laughed a lot, everyone was happy, for now. He didn't know what he'd want—what she'd want—tomorrow.

"I'll worry about the expense," Sam said, keeping the details to himself.

The past few days had been eye-opening. He was a better cook than Lizzie—which wasn't saying much. She didn't talk all the time after all. He had learned how to silence her, when he wanted silence. He knew very well how to change the track of her thoughts no matter where they might take her. She was single-minded once he got her naked. So was he, to be honest.

It had been a very long time since he'd spent this much time with any one woman. He'd known it was possible that one day he'd meet a woman who was different from the rest, one who made him want to stay, but he certainly hadn't expected it to be Lizzie. He hadn't expected that after almost a week he was not at all tired of her, that he still walked into a room and looked at her and could think of nothing else but getting her clothes—and his—off. He still woke up at night with her lying beside him and couldn't help but wake her with his hands and his mouth until they found better pursuits than sleep.

Lucky for him, she hadn't yet thought of a way to approach Jenna without scaring the kid or saying too much. Her days had been busy with another painting job—for which she had either Danny or Mike as an assistant—and Sam kept her busy enough at night.

Would he be lucky enough that she'd simply change her mind about trying to form a relationship with Jenna Aldridge?

Unlikely. Lizzie was single-minded out of bed, too.

"It's been five days since anything happened," Danny said. "No more wild gunshots, no menacing phone calls or strange cars on the street. If there's no more excitement for Lizzie or for the ex-Mrs. Travers, how long do we keep this up?"

"As long as it takes."

"You do know that if there's nothing more, we're done. We have no proof, no solid suspects, and unless the police reports give us something, which is unlikely, then we've hit a wall and have nowhere to go."

Sam almost snapped, but he knew too well that Danny was right. Someone had been trying to scare him. That someone had succeeded. Was that the end of it? A couple of gunshots and it was over?

Marilyn buzzed him on the desk intercom. "Boss, there's an Officer Talbot here. Can I send him in?"

Talbot, the young officer from Friday night's excitement at Dottie Ann's. God, he hoped the kid wasn't here to shake his hand again. "Send him in."

Talbot didn't linger in the outer office. A couple of seconds after Sam gave the okay, the kid walked into the room. The uniformed officer looked sharp, on edge, and he clutched a manila envelope in one hand. "I owe you, Travers, so I wanted to deliver this report personally."

"Something interesting there?" Sam asked, offering his hand.

"Oh, yeah, definitely interesting. First of all, the bullet from the second shooting didn't match the two from the first. The details are in the report."

The hairs on the back of Sam's neck stood up as he reached for the offered file.

"Second," Talbot said, his eyes darkening, "I finally got in touch with the last of your ex-wife's neighbors. She was a hard woman to catch at home, but I went by this morning and got her. She says—" the kid actually blushed "—she says your ex fired that shot into her own house."

Sam was quiet for a moment. Danny and Talbot watched him, waiting. Finally he asked, "Have you talked to Dottie Ann?"

"No, sir," Talbot said. "I wanted to touch base with you first."

"Was anyone with you when you talked to the neighbor?"

Talbot shook his head. "And I haven't filed a report on it, either. I wasn't sure how you'd want this handled, and it's not like your ex shot into someone else's house. Now, if the same bullet had also been fired into the other house that would be another matter, but that's not the case."

No, that was not the case at all. Sam returned the official file with the ballistics report inside to Talbot. Inside he was seething, but he worked to maintain his cool. It was that or hit the ceiling. "Thanks for keeping this quiet. I appreciate the head's up. If you don't mind, I'll handle it myself." He'd love to hand his ex over to the cops, but it looked like he'd be taking care of Dottie Ann's problems one last time.

* * *

Lizzie's mind wandered as she rolled a layer of Cincinnati Claret onto the flawlessly smooth wall. The man who owned this house had asked for eggshell white, but the room didn't want to be boring eggshell white. It wanted to be alive and bright and *red*. This wasn't a bright red, like a child's crayon, it was a deep rich cranberry color that brought the wooden floors in this room to life. Maybe it would bring the dull man who'd hired her to life, too. Anything was possible.

If the client didn't like it she'd repaint, but so far no one had asked for a redo. She knew what she was doing.

Well, when it came to painting she knew what she was doing. The rest of her life was pretty much a mess. What else was new?

She still wasn't sure how to approach Jenna. Now that they'd met they could strike up a conversation if they "accidentally" ran into one another. Lizzie had played the meeting over and over in her mind. *How do you like the blue in your room? I love it! What are you doing here? Oh, just hanging out. Me, too! Wanna get a soda?* And so it would go. The *Your idiot stepfather is sending you to boarding school* conversation would come later. The problem was, Lizzie had no idea where Jenna hung out, and she really didn't want to become a stalker to find out. Sam probably had ways of digging up that information, but she knew how he felt about the matter and she didn't want to bring it up.

Besides, she had Sam problems as well as Jenna problems.

She loved him. Okay, she'd always loved him a little, but this was different. This was real. It was more than sex, not that the sex wasn't brilliant. She loved the Sam she knew today, not the memory of the young man he had once been, not a teenage girl's fantasy. She loved the way he touched her, the way he met her gaze so ardently, the way he watched television, the way he slept, the way he cooked for her, the way he took on the weight of the world…his world *and* hers. She loved it all. Less than a week of being truly together, and she couldn't imagine her life without Sam in it. The house would not be the same if he wasn't there every night and every morning. She didn't think she could bear a night alone; she'd so quickly come to need his heat and weight beside her on the bed.

That all sounded lovely and romantic and life altering, but she knew Sam didn't love her. Oh, he liked her well enough, and he certainly wanted her, but love wasn't in his heart or in his plans for the future.

Which kept her where she was, lost in a decadent and wonderful sort of limbo. Keeping Sam meant settling for less than she wanted…less than she or any other woman deserved. Letting him go would break her heart.

She had Mike with her today. He wasn't as experienced a painter as Danny, but he did well enough. Since nothing had happened in days—almost a week—he'd relaxed a bit and was no longer quite so on guard. Not that he'd ever been as intense as Sam. Still, he was big and brawny and armed, and if anyone was out to hurt or scare her they'd have a tough time getting past him.

Every girl needed a contingent of bodyguards now and then, she supposed. Hers was stellar.

When they finished and had packed away their supplies, Lizzie went searching for the man who'd hired her. Bill Fender was a thin, easily distracted computer nerd who worked at home in an office that was, yet again, eggshell white. Maybe if he loved the den, he'd hire her to fix up more rooms. If he hated what she'd done, she'd be back tomorrow to fix it, and man, painting over red would be a royal pain.

She led Fender into the den. He'd been in the middle of something on his computer and was not at all pleased to be interrupted. Did he always look so distracted and out of it? Did he live in that office of his?

Fender walked quickly, taking short but quick and anxious steps, obviously in a hurry to get back to his computer. He followed Lizzie into the den, and as soon as he saw the results of her work he came to a halt with a stutter step that almost threw him backward. "This is not what I asked you to do."

"I know," Lizzie said calmly. "And if it's not to your liking, I'll redo it. No extra charge to you, of course," she said when he shot her a puzzled glance. "It's just that color is my thing. I know color, I can feel it, and this room is more alive than it has ever been."

"It's red."

"It's Cincinnati Claret," she corrected gently. "Mr. Fender, do you—"

"Bill," he said, studying the walls with a critical eye. "Call me Bill."

"Okay." That was a good sign, she supposed. "Bill, do you ever bring women to your home?"

He looked at her oddly. "Sometimes."

"Do you sit in this room and talk or watch a movie on the TV or…whatever?"

"Sure."

"Imagine the reaction your lady friends will have when they walk into this room," she said softly. "This den no longer looks like every other den in the neighborhood. It's alive, it's trendy, it's hip."

Fender wrinkled his nose. "Does anyone say *hip* anymore?"

Lizzie sighed. "Probably not, but you get the idea. The man who lives here is on the edge, he's with it, he's a step above the other schmucks who don't care about their homes the way you do. A man who gives so much thought to the details of his home will also give the same consideration to the woman in his life, and trust me when I tell you, we notice."

Mike was suppressing a smile, forcing his lips into a tight line while his eyes danced.

Fender's face relaxed. He stepped back and surveyed the room with a new and more appreciative eye. "I like it," he said. "It's different, but in a good way. There's no need to redo anything." He nodded his head in a gesture of approval. "While you're here, could you take a look at the bedroom and my office? Just tell me what you think. Maybe they'd benefit from a bit of color."

Lizzie smiled. This sort of thing happened a lot.

After she and Mike had checked out the rooms in question, and she'd made suggestions, they headed for the truck. Fender said he'd call and set up a time for her to paint those rooms, and she was pretty sure he would. He definitely wasn't a do-it-yourself guy.

It was late afternoon, and the day was a pretty one. Sam wouldn't be at the house for a couple of hours, and she didn't want to sit there and think. She had way too much to think about. As she cranked up the truck she glanced at Mike, who looked as if he was about to doze off in the passenger seat. "We're going to make a stop on the way home," she said.

He sat up straight, instantly alert. "Where?"

"I'm just going to make a quick stop to see if a friend is around."

"Oh." He relaxed and leaned back in his seat.

Oh, indeed. If Sam knew what she was up to he wouldn't be pleased. Did he think she'd given up on Jenna, even though she'd told him—once or twice— that she had not? She headed for the school. Last week Jenna had been late getting home because she'd had a Thursday-afternoon school soccer practice. Maybe that was a weekly thing. She could hope!

Sam pulled up to the curb, noticing that Dottie Ann's front window had been replaced and the house looked as if nothing had happened here. Which was as it should be, since nothing really had happened here.

If the bullets from the two shootings had matched, he'd think his ex had found out that Lizzie was back and they were seeing one another and she'd taken drastic measures to keep them apart, then fired into her own house to throw suspicion into another direction. But Dottie Ann wasn't smart enough to think of changing guns, so that was out.

He knocked on the door, knowing she'd be at home. Dottie Ann didn't work. She'd relied on her two ex-husbands to keep her solvent and taken care of. Thank goodness he had stopped paying alimony when she'd remarried, and that her second husband had done well enough for himself to keep the ex fed and housed and in shoes.

She answered the door with a smile on her face. "Sam, what a nice surprise. Come in."

He didn't dare. He was on the verge of seriously

losing his temper, and though he'd never before hit a woman—he was tempted. "I'll stay right here. I just have a message I wanted to deliver in person."

"Oh," she said, looking alarmed. "Is it about the case? Did you find out who's been trying to scare the women in your life?"

"Cut the crap. A neighbor saw you. I don't know what the hell you were thinking when you shot into your own house."

"No one saw me," she said as she blushed. "It was dark and I was wearing black and I stood on the other side of those bushes where it would be almost impossible…"

She really was a numbskull. "*Almost* is the key word there. You have twenty seconds to explain to me what happened. If I'm not satisfied, then the police and your insurance company are going to find out what I just found out, and then you'll be in real trouble."

Now she paled. "I…I…"

"Tick tock," he said to spur her on.

"I know a girl who dates a guy who sometimes works for you," Dottie Ann said, her voice quick and almost breathless, "and I heard that Lizzie was around and someone had shot at her house and you were livid and protecting her and it just made me so mad. Lizzie Porter, after all these years. That little mousy kid was going to get you after all. And here I've been doing everything I could to get your attention and you won't give me the time of day! I thought maybe you'd be livid that someone had shot at *me,* and if we had some time together I could get you back."

"You want me back?" Sam asked, horrified. He'd seen the signs, but he'd thought that had just been Dottie Ann being Dottie Ann.

"Yes! It was a mistake to leave when I did." Her eyes got big and she balled her fists. "I was scared, and there was all that ugly publicity, and I didn't even know if you'd ever have a decent job again when it was all said and done, and…and you changed. Now you're successful, and you still look good, and we're both alone so it makes perfect sense to get back together, only you refuse to see sense."

Sam hadn't always seen sense where Dottie Ann was concerned, but he saw now. He took a step back, away from the frantic woman. "Don't call me anymore," he said. "If something breaks, call your other ex or hire a handyman. I'm done."

"But…"

"Call me again and I'll hand over what I have to the police. You have no idea what kind of trouble you could be in."

Dottie Ann stepped away from him, body and eyes stiff. "You are such a bastard." She slammed the door before he could respond, and Sam gratefully headed for his car. It was entirely possible that the gunshot which had been fired into Lizzie's house was nothing more than a random drive-by. No one was targeting the women in his life. Since there had been no more hint of real trouble in the past week, no phone calls or disturbances at the house, it was also unlikely that anyone had been targeting Lizzie.

He headed for her house, anxious to see her, anxious to tell her that the threat was over—that there hadn't ever been a real threat. He wanted to share the news in person, not by cell phone.

A realization he hadn't expected stole a moment of his relief. Lizzie no longer needed his protection, but he wasn't ready to let her go. He didn't want to move out of her house and go back to the way things had been…and that was a complication he hadn't seen coming.

Chapter 13

Sure enough, there was a group of girls on the field where Lizzie had seen Jenna's team playing. They weren't in uniform, but she immediately picked out Jenna's ponytail, swaying as she ran and took control of the ball. The young girl moved with such grace! She was truly beautiful.

Lizzie surveyed the area, and was relieved to see an oval track to one side of the field. A couple of women were already out there, getting their exercise for the day by walking briskly in a loop. They had the bodies of women who walked—or ran—often, and were wearing formfitting clothes that weren't good for anything but exercising.

Lizzie didn't have workout clothes with her—okay, she didn't *own* workout clothes—but what she was wearing would do. She opened her door and hopped out of the truck. Mike did the same.

"I can walk alone," she said.

"Now you're walking?" he asked. "I thought you were here to meet a friend?"

Without a word, since she didn't want to lie, she gestured nonspecifically to the track and the field with a sweeping hand. Mike looked at the exercising women and gave a quiet "oh." When Lizzie took her first steps toward the track, he followed.

This would never do. Lizzie spun on him. "We really need to talk about private matters. It's, uh, girl stuff," she said in a lowered, almost mysterious voice.

"Oh," Mike said again, looking and sounding suitably terrified of the ambiguous "girl stuff."

"You can see me from here," Lizzie said with a smile. "I don't plan to be long." Even if she didn't get a chance to speak to Jenna, she could at least watch her for a while. Maybe that would be enough, for now.

Leaving Mike behind, Lizzie picked up her pace. Since Mike would be watching, she'd have to say at least a few words to one of the women on the track. Didn't matter which one. Her eyes cut to the soccer field often. A few parents were in attendance, even though it was just a practice, but naturally Connelly was nowhere to be seen. The driver would probably be taking Jenna home today. Maybe some people would be thrilled to have their own driver, but Lizzie thought it was kinda sad for a twelve-year-old.

She stepped onto the track and increased her pace until she was directly beside one of the women. "Hi," Lizzie said brightly. "Beautiful day, isn't it?"

The walker, a blonde who had an incredibly toned body that was shown off to its full advantage in tight black spandex, returned the smile. "It is that." Her eyes remained fixed forward, on the track.

"I haven't walked here before," Lizzie said. "Is it all right for the public to use this track?"

"Sure. Not during school hours and not if there's a school practice or meet, of course," the blonde added. She finally glanced to the side and looked Lizzie up and down. "That's not what I'd call your usual walking gear."

"I came straight from work," Lizzie said.

"Painter?" the blonde asked.

"How did you guess?" They both laughed, which would look very good for Mike's benefit.

Lizzie divided her attention between the soccer practice and her walking companion, who introduced herself as Rebecca. She had a daughter on the soccer team, and it just so happened she'd been thinking about painting the interior of her house. Lizzie half listened as Rebecca spoke about the rooms in her home, what colors she'd been contemplating, how her husband wanted boring and she wanted something with pizzazz. Rebecca eyed the splatters of red paint on Lizzie's coveralls as she said the word *pizzazz*.

Too soon practice was over, and Rebecca's pace slowed. She stopped, twisted her torso a couple of times as if working out a few kinks and asked for a business card. Lizzie reached into a deep pocket of her overalls and complied. Even though they likely had nothing in common, she liked Rebecca. She wouldn't mind at all working for her, for a while.

A redheaded girl ran to Rebecca, a smile on her flushed and freckled face. The smile was returned, and there was so much love on Rebecca's face, Lizzie felt a moment's envy. Her own mother had never been so openly caring and tuned in. This was the kind of mother Jenna deserved.

Lizzie took her gaze from the mother and daughter to watch as Jenna headed off the field, loping with long, coltish legs, ponytail swinging, her eyes on the parking lot. So much for a chance meeting.

A teammate called Jenna's name, and the young girl turned to wave. When she did, she saw Lizzie. Lizzie knew she'd been seen because Jenna's step stuttered and she slowed, and then she turned around and jogged directly toward the track.

"Hey!" Jenna said when she got close. "I thought that was you!"

Lizzie smiled. "Hi, Jenna. How are you doing?"

"Pretty good. *Love* the blue you painted my room. It's so peaceful and bright at the same time! Darryl wanted to paint over it, but I wouldn't let him. It's just *too* perfect."

Rebecca's eyes lit up and she looked at Lizzie with raised eyebrows and a hint of a smile. "You worked for Darryl Connelly?"

"For a few days," Lizzie said, hoping the woman didn't call Connelly for a reference. That could be ugly….

"She's awesome," Jenna said. "You should see the blue she painted my room! That color changed everything, and it's *so* much better than before. And she didn't get even a drop of paint on anything." Her eyes met Lizzie's. "How's Homer?"

"He's fine." Lizzie smiled. Parents and players were drifting away; this conversation wouldn't last much longer. "Y'all are very good," she said, glancing from the redhead to Jenna, so as not to appear too fixated on her sister. "Is there a game this weekend?"

"No. Next week is spring break," the redhead said. She looked at Jenna. "Are you going anywhere?"

"We're going to our place in Orange Beach for the entire week." Jenna wrinkled her Charlie-like nose. "Darryl is taking Heather, so I'll be on my own a lot. Which is not too terrible," she clarified brightly. "The house is right on the beach, and I love to swim, and I plan to pack a lot of books."

"I love to read!" Lizzie said, glad to have yet another commonality with Jenna, no matter how small.

"Me, too." Jenna glanced toward the parking lot, where her car and driver waited. "I have to go." She looked at Lizzie. "Games will pick up after spring break, if you really want to come watch us."

"I do."

Jenna ran toward the parking lot. "Call me and I'll get you the schedule!"

Lizzie watched her sister run. It wasn't exactly the conversation she'd planned, and they had not been alone, but it was nice. Very nice.

Rebecca waved and said goodbye, following her own daughter to the parking lot. That was when Lizzie noticed Mike watching closely.

He held his cell phone in one meaty hand. Not good. Dollars to doughnuts he was talking to Sam, who would *not* be happy to hear where they'd stopped after work.

Sam opened the front door before Lizzie had a chance to get out of the truck she pulled so gently into her driveway. Mike hopped out of the passenger seat, nodded to Sam, took one look at his face and headed for his car, which was parked at the curb. Mike had already gotten an earful over the phone, when Sam had called to ask when Lizzie would be home.

Home. This was not his home, though he now carried

a key to the front door on his key chain. A warning inched up Sam's neck, a buzz alerting him instinctively that all was not well. Lizzie smiled at him as she walked toward the front door, but there was less joy than usual in her eyes. She knew he was pissed—surely Mike had told her that much.

"Mike said you have news that you want to deliver in person," she said as she walked up the front porch steps.

"I do. What the hell were you doing at Jenna's school?"

She met him, went up on her toes to kiss him all too briefly, then dropped back down as they stepped inside. "Can't I have the good news first?"

"No," he snapped.

"Blackmail," she muttered as she dropped her much-abused oversize purse on the entry hall table. "Fine, I remembered that Jenna has soccer practice on Thursday afternoons, and I decided to drop by to see her."

"I thought we agreed that wasn't a good idea."

"You agreed," she said. "Actually, there is no such thing as agreeing with yourself, is there? So, no, there was no agreement. I haven't made a secret of the fact that I don't like Darryl Connelly or his self-obsessed woman and that I don't think Jenna is being treated as well as she should be, and I'm not going to give up."

He glared at her; his glare didn't have much effect on her these days. It was hard to put fear into a woman when she knew damn well that with a smile and a crook of her finger she could have him wherever and whenever she wanted him.

"She's my sister, Sam. I feel it to the pit of my soul, I see it in her face, I hear it in her voice."

"If she was in a less than ideal situation…" he began.

"Not being loved unconditionally *is* less than ideal, in my opinion." She faced him, arms crossed over her chest. "So, what's the good news?"

"Dottie Ann shot into her own living room."

Lizzie's eyes widened and she blinked twice. "That psycho shot at my house because she knew you were here?"

"No," Sam said calmly. "She shot at her own house to get my sorry ass over there, which means it's entirely possible that either the shooting here was random or someone was really unhappy because you painted their once-manly office pink." He couldn't stay mad at her, not when she was looking at him like this.

A smile tugged at her lips. "No more round-the-clock bodyguard?"

Sam shook his head. Though he hated to leave Lizzie on her own, hated for her to be out of his sight—to be honest, out of his *control*—for one minute, there was no longer reliable evidence that she was a target. It wasn't as if he could protect her forever, no matter how right it seemed at the moment.

Lizzie's smile died slowly. She looked at him hard, a host of unspoken questions in her eyes. *Will you stay? Is it over? Are you walking—or running—out of my life now?*

He unfastened the straps of her stained and faded overalls. Since the overalls were horribly oversize they immediately dropped to the floor, an expanse of paint-splattered denim pooling at her feet. Beneath she was entirely female, from the snug white tee that hugged her curves, to the pink panties with an edge of lace, to the deliciously long legs.

He wanted to ask her why she hid her beauty behind

baggy clothes that were always a couple of sizes too large for her. He wanted to ask her why she didn't find a thrill in dressing up and buying shoes the way other women did. He'd seen her dressed to kill once, for their first date, so he knew she could—when it suited her.

But he was much too busy to ask questions now. Maybe later.

It all happened so naturally, without thought or word or instruction of any kind. Lizzie stepped out of her shoes and let Sam lift her out of a puddle of overalls to carry her up the stairs. Just days ago he had made love to her there, against the wall, because to stumble a few more steps to her bedroom would've taken too long. Their desire for one another hadn't dimmed, but the urgency had faded, a little. He had no trouble making it to her bed and dropping her there. She landed with a bounce that didn't last because Sam was almost immediately on top of her, heavy and warm and anxious, just as she was. Her body stretched beneath his, hungry and restless, and yet also content. This was fine, to be wanted, and to want. To hop on the roller coaster that was Sam Travers and ride it out to the fabulous end. She could almost lift her arms above her head and scream in sheer delight. Sam Travers, thrill ride.

She started undressing him while he gave all his attention to her neck, kissing her there while he pushed her shirt up. He apparently had a thing for her neck, and she certainly wasn't complaining. She'd be naked soon, she knew, so it was only fair that he be in the same state of undress. Heaven above, she loved the feel of his skin against hers almost as much as she loved the sensation of him filling her, riding her to the end that drove them.

They twisted and turned and reached, but there was no awkwardness in their moves. She got him mostly undressed; he stripped her naked, kissing and stroking along the way. She reached for him and he filled her hand, hot and hard. She stroked, lost in a haze of longing and pleasure, riding the roller coaster without the annoyance of thinking about anything but how wonderful having Sam in her bed felt.

Had she ever really accused him of being unfamiliar with prep work? How foolish of her. He was a master of prep work, a man with an eye to detail. A few days together, and he knew exactly how and where to touch her to bring her to a fever pitch. He knew where all her buttons were, and he pushed them well. By the time he thrust inside her she was breathless and aching and ravenous. She cried out a little as he filled her, and then the ride truly began. He pushed inside her, hard and fast. There was no gentleness in this coming together, no softness. They were driven by primitive urges, operating on instinct as they sought the ultimate pleasure.

A pleasure they found together, too soon. Lizzie cried out again; she darn near screamed, and when she felt Sam's release she savored it as much as she'd savored her own.

And the words tumbled out, as unbidden and unplanned as the way her hips had risen and gyrated to bring him closer and deeper.

"I love you."

Sam's hips continued to move, but gently now. His lips trailed across her throat. He didn't say a word, and as the seconds passed Lizzie's heart began to sink and sink and sink. She'd known he didn't love her. She'd known it all along. But to have the evidence revealed to her so clearly hurt more than she'd thought it would. She should've kept her mouth shut.

But she'd never been very good at keeping her mouth shut.

Sam was still on top of her, still inside her, and her heart continued to plummet. Just minutes ago she'd told Sam that her sister deserved unconditional love. Didn't she deserve the same? Didn't she deserve to have a man in her life who truly loved her? With Sam she would always wonder when he was going to leave. Not if, but when. She knew this wouldn't last. The question was *when.*

The longer this maddening and wonderful and unexpected and shattering affair lasted, the more it would hurt when it was over.

Lizzie closed her eyes. She tipped her head back and allowed Sam to continue to kiss her throat. He wouldn't see the tears that leaked from her eyes and dribbled onto the pillow. She didn't make a sound to alert him to her distress. They would shower together now. When the long, hot shower was done, they'd get halfway dressed and have dinner, either takeout or something Sam threw together. And eventually they would come to this bed again.

He had to go; he had to get out of her life.

But heaven above, not tonight.

Chapter 14

Sam was usually up before Lizzie, so he was surprised to wake alone in her bed. He reached out and ran his fingers over her pillow. The sheets were warm; they still held her scent. Maybe she was downstairs making breakfast.

That thought spurred him out of bed. Lizzie was a great painter, she was a whiz in bed, she was smart and beautiful and funny and determined.

But she couldn't cook to save her life.

He didn't hear her in the kitchen as he headed down the stairs wearing nothing but a pair of boxers. If she was cooking she'd need serious help. He smelled the coffee; she did know how to make decent coffee, but that was about it. Maybe he'd awakened in time to stave off disaster.

He called her name before he stepped into the kitchen, then was surprised to find the bright room empty. The coffeepot was almost full. Sitting next to it, propped up on a coffee mug, sat a folded sheet of paper.

His stomach hit the floor.

This was about last night, he imagined, about the moment when she'd said those three words in the excitement of the moment. He should've said something in response, he supposed, but had thought it better just to ignore the lapse. Surely she regretted blurting out "I love you" while her body and his shuddered.

He carefully opened the note, and stood in the kitchen reading it. Twice.

Dear Sam,

I don't regret anything. Not that I said I love you, not what we've had these past few days. But we both know you and I don't want the same things from a relationship. The sex has been great, but it's not enough, not for me. I deserve more, and if I stay with you I'll never have it. You're too tempting. I can't look at you and walk away, which is why you're getting a cowardly note instead of a confrontation that might spoil the memory of what we've had. It's best this way. Pack your stuff (what little there is) and take it with you, and leave your key in the silverware drawer. I don't know when I'll be back, but when I do come home it would be best if everything of yours is gone.

Thanks for keeping an eye on me when it looked like things were getting ugly. It's nice to know no one was really taking potshots at me, but while we thought it was possible, you were the best. Thank the guys for me, too, especially

Danny and Mike. They both have painter's assistant jobs waiting for them if they ever get tired of working for you. Less pay, but I'm sure I'm a more pleasant boss than you are. (Sorry, my sad attempt at humor is falling flat this morning. I just don't feel very funny at the moment.)

I love you, I thank you, and I don't ever want to see you again. I guess that's all I really needed to say, but I write the way I talk, too long and too complicated and not knowing when to stop. Take care.

Love,
Lizzie

Sam held the sheet of paper in his hands as the minutes ticked past. Why was he surprised? This couldn't have ended any other way. Lizzie was a marriage-and-babies woman, and he was a don't-tie-me-down man. It was bound to end sooner or later, and sooner was better—at least for Lizzie. Lucky for him, he didn't even have to watch her cry. No, he only had to see the evidence of her tears on the note he clutched in one hand.

The trip to Orange Beach hadn't taken quite as long as Lizzie had planned. Her truck rumbled into the hotel parking lot before noon. It probably wasn't even check-in time yet, but it wouldn't hurt to make sure she could get a room. She had a lot of investigating to do this afternoon, phone calls to make, arrangements of the most secretive sort to organize. Sam probably could've found out in a matter of minutes where Connelly's beach house was and if they had live-in help and whether or not the beach where Jenna was likely to hang out was private or public. She'd have to work for her info, but she was good with people, so all she had to do was meet some locals and ask some innocent-sounding questions that weren't really innocent at all. She didn't need Sam for this. She didn't need him for anything anymore.

Lizzie had cried some over leaving Sam behind, but she hadn't cried endlessly. That wasn't her way. She was going to do her best to concentrate on Jenna for now, to plan the best way to get some time with her sister before deciding what to do next.

She knew what she *wanted* to do, but kidnapping wouldn't look very good on her record if she decided to try for custody. No, she'd have to be a bit smoother than that.

The hotel she checked in to was touristy and tacky and less than spectacular, and still, Lizzie thought herself lucky to get the last available room for spring break. The air in the dim space smelled a little musty, and the pink-and-green bedspread and pictures were woefully out of style, and the walls…oh, the walls! But there was a bed, as well as a bathroom that was dated but clean. There was a television and a sturdy lock on the door that opened directly onto the parking lot. She'd stop at the grocery store for Lysol, bug spray and decent lightbulbs, and she'd be set for the week.

As she started unpacking her overnight bag—which was filled with clothes she'd snagged out of the laundry room near dawn that morning, being too cowardly to chance opening dresser drawers in the room where Sam slept—a few tears popped up again. She pushed the tears and the hint of regret back and looked ahead. Only ahead.

She had no other place to look. Living in the past would only ruin her life.

As if it wasn't already pretty well wrecked.

Sam did as Lizzie had requested and left. It was her house, after all, and she had every right to kick him out. He drove to an upscale condo that didn't feel at all like home at the moment, and after a while he attempted to call Lizzie on her cell. Just to make sure she was okay. He dialed three numbers and then thought better of the plan and flipped the phone shut. She wanted a clean break; he would give her one.

He went to work, not saying a word to anyone about the reason for his bad mood. There was work enough to keep him occupied, but his mind was never entirely away from Lizzie. When he left the office a couple of hours early, his employees who had the misfortune to be working in-office today were all relieved to see him go. He couldn't say that he blamed them.

Driving past Lizzie's house was a bad idea, but he wanted to make sure she got home okay. He wouldn't stop. When he saw her truck in the driveway, he'd feel better. For the first time he felt grateful for the fact that Charlie had kept his single-car garage so filled with junk that there was no room for a vehicle there.

He hadn't thought about Charlie enough lately. Charlie would tell him that Lizzie deserved better—either before or after the old man kicked his sorry ass. Hell, he missed his old partner, even though they'd not been close in past years. For the first time since he'd heard the news of Charlie's passing, he felt a rush of grief. The world was a sadder place without Charlie Porter in it.

The first time he drove by Lizzie's house and there was no truck in the driveway, he wasn't alarmed. Lizzie often worked late. She might've decided to eat out instead of—heaven forbid—cooking. He stopped for a cup of coffee and then drove down her street again. Nothing. He stopped at the grocery store for a few cans of soup, since he didn't have much in the way of food at his place. After that she still wasn't home.

The fourth time he drove by and saw the house still dark and the driveway empty, he got pissed. Parking down the street a ways, he pinned his eyes to Lizzie's house.

What the hell was he doing? It was best that their relationship end; he'd been telling himself that all day. Yes, he missed her; yes, he wished they'd had more time, but that didn't mean he'd fooled himself into thinking what they had was long-term. He didn't do long-term, and she knew it. So why was he staking out her house, anxious—frantic—to see her, to know she was safe?

As the minutes ticked past slowly, he tried to tell himself that he'd do the same for any former client, but he couldn't make himself buy it, not for a moment.

Her creepy neighbor, thin and beady eyed and dressed in what looked for all the world like ragged hand-me-downs, came out to collect his mail. With mail in hand the neighbor glanced at Lizzie's house, and after a short hesitation he walked toward her driveway. Garet Miles looked toward the dark house while he walked, then he stopped in front of Lizzie's mailbox and opened it slowly, peeking inside.

Working on instinct, Sam jumped out of the car and ran. Son of a bitch. First the phone calls and now this. Garet heard pounding footsteps and lifted his head, just in time to see Sam vault toward him. They both landed hard on the asphalt, but the creepy guy took the worst of it, since he was unprepared and on the bottom.

"What the hell are you doing snooping in Lizzie's mailbox?" Sam shouted.

Garet wheezed and coughed and tried to push Sam away. He had about as much strength in his thin arms as an eight-year-old might. "Get off me, you thug. I'm going to call the police! We have neighborhood watch and I'm sure someone is watching this attack! Get *off!*"

Sam didn't move an inch. "What are you doing with Lizzie's mail?" Which was presently spread across the street—along with Garet's. He hadn't been able to hold on as he'd fallen to the ground.

"Lizzie asked me to collect her mail until she gets back! If you want it, you can have it all! Go ahead, take it!"

Sam didn't say anything for a minute. The wind kicked up and blew away a few envelopes.

"Come *on,*" Garet wailed. "Let me get my mail. My electric bill is in there!"

Chagrined, pissed at himself for overreacting, Sam jumped up and started gathering the envelopes and flyers that were blowing about. Odds were the creepy guy was telling the truth—which meant Sam was an ass, and also meant that Lizzie wouldn't be back tonight. When he had all the mail gathered, Sam returned to the neighbor, who was now sitting on Lizzie's curb trying to catch his breath.

"Sorry, man," he said. "I thought you were up to no good."

Garet wheezed. "I've met possessive boyfriends before, buddy, but you take the cake."

"I'm not…" Sam started to say *a boyfriend,* then changed his mind. "I'm not possessive."

Shaken as he was, Garet started to laugh. "Yeah, right. I did think Lizzie had better sense than to go for the Neanderthal type, but I guess I was wrong."

Deflated, Sam sat on the curb. He didn't even bother to argue with Garet about the "Neanderthal" comment. "So, when is Lizzie coming back?"

"You've got it bad," Garet said with an evil, breathless cackle.

"I don't have anything, bad or otherwise."

The thin man shrugged. "If you say so. Anyway, Lizzie said she might be gone awhile."

"I don't suppose she told you where she was headed."

"Nope."

Sam's stomach sank. It felt as if a rock had settled there. He'd disappointed her and she'd run. In truth, he shouldn't have expected any other reaction. Had she left town or just gone to an apartment or a hotel? If she was close by, why would she ask Garet to get her mail? Maybe because she knew Sam Travers better than he realized, and she wouldn't be at all surprised to see him sitting here now, breathless and apologetic and curious as hell.

She wouldn't get far from Jenna, he knew that. Maybe if he staked out the Connelly house he'd get a lead on where Lizzie had disappeared to.

It was a bad idea. He should let Lizzie go, as she'd asked him to do. He should read that freakin' tearstained letter until he got it through his thick skull that they weren't going to work out.

But letting Lizzie go was tougher than he'd imagined it would be. She was everything he didn't want in a woman. She asked more of him than any other woman ever had or would, and he should be glad it was over. But as he sat on the curb with her breathless, shaken neighbor, he knew that nothing was over, not where Lizzie was concerned.

People loved to talk, and Lizzie was definitely in the mood to listen. It had been easy to find out which beach house belonged to Darryl Connelly. There were no live-in servants in the two-story yellow house, which looked like an oversize cottage on stilts. A huge deck over-looked the gulf. Much as Connelly would've liked for the beachfront to be private, it was not, though it was far enough away from the towering condos to keep the crowds from settling in there. There were equally nice cottages sitting nearby, and while there was no mob here, there was regular foot traffic along the shoreline.

The locals she talked to at the small shops along the highway were vocal about the way they didn't much like Darryl, how they'd watched Jenna grow into a fine young woman in spite of her stepfather and how they laughed at Heather when her back was turned.

Lizzie considered them good people with excellent instincts.

And now she sat on the beach, wearing a big floppy hat and the two-piece bathing suit she'd picked up at a local shop, seriously overpaying for the too-teeny black bikini. It wasn't the sort of bathing suit she'd normally choose, but her choices had been the black bikini or a bright flowery one-piece that was four sizes too large. While she usually bought her clothes a size or two too large, with a bathing suit that wasn't an option. She'd placed herself on a beach towel a little way down from the Connelly house, not wanting to be too obvious. Now and then she scanned the pages of the mystery novel she'd purchased at the grocery store, but none of the words made sense to her. Her mind was most definitely elsewhere.

Out of the corner of her eye she could see the house she was watching, and occasionally she turned as if studying the shoreline, fully taking in the deck, watching for a sign that the house was occupied. She'd thought that Connelly and his girlfriend and Jenna might've come in last night, since it wasn't a long drive, but now she wondered if they were coming at all. Maybe they'd wait a day or two. Maybe their plans had changed, and they weren't coming. Wouldn't that just be her luck?

She didn't even make a decent stalker.

A few times Lizzie left her towel and book behind and walked into the gulf, even though the water was cool this time of year. She liked the feel of the surf on her feet and her calves, the way the sand squished between her toes. In a couple of months the water temperature would be perfect. As the day dragged endlessly onward she reapplied her heavy-duty sunscreen often, not wanting to blister in the name of spying on Jenna. Maybe it was only March, but that didn't mean burning wasn't possible. She'd never been able to tan properly and had suffered more than one sunburn.

As she waited, Lizzie had lots of time to think. If she was going to make herself a part of Jenna's life, she needed a plan. She really didn't want to turn the girl's well-ordered life upside down, but Jenna needed someone in her life who loved her completely, who screamed at her soccer games and gave her big hugs and made a fuss over every good grade. Before too long she'd need someone to vet the boys who were sure to come sniffing around, and to scare away the ones who were entirely unsuitable. Too bad Sam wouldn't be around. He'd be great at scaring off unacceptable suitors with a look, and maybe with an "accidental" display of his gun.

Lizzie returned her gaze to the gently lapping water, trying to harden her heart. She didn't need Sam; she had a Taser.

Finally, to her great relief, she saw activity on the deck of the Connelly beach house—and still, she wasn't sure how to proceed. A relationship with Jenna was necessary. She craved it almost as much as she craved Sam—maybe more, but in a totally different way. In a way she didn't like, she needed Sam; in a way she could not explain, she knew Jenna needed her.

Could she be brave enough, strong enough, to make a relationship with Jenna happen, in spite of all the reasons for not taking that path?

Not long after she saw the activity she'd been waiting for, Jenna came bopping onto the beach, alone. The girl's bathing suit was a one-piece in three shades of purple and had probably cost ten times what Lizzie had paid for her suit. The beach towel Jenna carried matched the suit, as did her flip-flops. Her long hair was pulled into a high, thick ponytail.

Butterflies danced in Lizzie's stomach. She adored her little sister, a child she barely knew. And she still didn't know what to say. Maybe she'd say nothing. Maybe she'd get up and walk away, running like a coward once again.

Jenna looked up and down the beach, her gaze coming to rest on Lizzie. A hand came up to shade her eyes, and after a moment, she waved and took a few steps in Lizzie's direction. She looked puzzled for a moment, and then she smiled widely. The poor child hadn't yet developed the self-protective skills that would warn her if she happened to run into the same person too often. Not that she needed to be protected from Lizzie, but any child who had a ridiculously rich stepfather should be warned to be on the lookout for strangers—or near strangers—and odd coincidences.

"Hi," Jenna said brightly when she was close. "This is so weird, seeing you here."

"Definitely weird," Lizzie said, trying to appear casual when she felt anything but on the inside. She had to remember, no matter what she wanted, all that mattered was Jenna and what the girl wanted and needed. Did she need a big sister, even if she didn't know of their blood relationship?

"We have a house here," Jenna said, turning to point at the yellow cottage. "Where are you staying?"

"At a ratty hotel," Lizzie said, and then she smiled. She wasn't going to ruin a few precious minutes with her sister by worrying herself sick over what she should or should not do. She would listen to her heart and dismiss all fears. "My room is pink and green, and the walls are in serious need of a coat of paint. They're the most awful shade of bubblegum pink, and they're over-due for a touch-up by, oh, ten years or so." She patted the sand beside her. "Sit. It's a gorgeous day, and I don't want to think about the hotel's horrendous walls."

Jenna laid out her towel. "If you don't mind."

"Not at all."

"My name is Jenna, by the way." She looked sheepish. "In case you forgot."

"I didn't forget." She wondered if that was a hint. "I'm Lizzie."

Jenna smiled. "I remember. Where's Homer?"

Lizzie shrugged her shoulders, trying to appear casual. "We broke up."

"Why?"

"It just wasn't working out. He's…"

When Lizzie faltered, at a loss as to how to explain, Jenna said, "He's cute, for an old dude, but that doesn't mean he makes a good boyfriend."

"That's true." Old dude? Sam would be mortified.

"And honestly, Homer? What kind of name is that? If my boyfriend was named Homer I'd suggest that he change his name or else I'd give him a really cool nickname. Spike, maybe, or Angel." She shrugged her shoulders. "I'm kind of obsessed with *Buffy* reruns at the moment."

Lizzie looked at Jenna in horror. "You have a *boyfriend?*"

"Not yet."

Relief rushed through Lizzie, and for a moment she realized what it must feel like to be a parent. "Good. You're way too young."

Jenna sighed. "You sound like my stepfather."

Good heavens, she hadn't thought she and Connelly would ever agree on anything! Especially where Jenna was concerned. Maybe he did have a few adequate parenting skills after all.

She and Jenna sat there and talked, the conversation natural and easy. Jenna glanced at Lizzie's mystery novel and mentioned the young adult vampire novel she was currently reading. That led into several minutes of discussion on favorite books. Somehow, in a short amount of time they touched on soccer, the weather, Lizzie's job, movies and shoes. It was everything Lizzie had dreamed of, and more, and she didn't have to do anything but sit there and listen, responding when it was appropriate. Sometimes they talked over one another in their excitement, but there wasn't a hint of awkwardness.

They were so engrossed in their conversation, neither of them realized Connelly was approaching until he stood over them, blocking the sun.

"Jenna, I have asked you time and again to stay where I can see you from the house. Don't make me worry."

"Sorry!" Jenna stood and snapped up her towel. "I saw Lizzie and I had to get closer to, you know, see if it was really her, and it was! Well, duh. You can see her for yourself. We got to talking and I didn't even think. I should've asked her to move down a ways so you could see us."

Connelly's hard eyes were glued to Lizzie. "What were you two talking about?"

"Just stuff." Jenna shrugged. "Her ex-boyfriend and movies and Buffy—she saw it when it was *new*—and ice cream and…what else? Anyway, just stuff. Oh, I have an idea! Lizzie is staying in an awful hotel. Pink and green! Can you imagine? She should stay with us. We have a guest room. It would be so much nicer for her, and she could keep us *both* company since Heather couldn't make it."

"I wouldn't want to impose," Lizzie said, her mouth going dry.

"It would be no imposition at all," Darryl said, his eyes continuing to bore into her. For a moment he let his eyes wander over her mostly exposed body, and she wished for a cover-up—or her overalls. It was men like this one that made Lizzie so comfortable in clothes that hid whatever womanly assets she might possess. She didn't want to be like her mother or the worst of the women Charlie had brought home when he'd started dating again—not that she had all that much to show off.

Besides, it was easier to hide than it was to confront. Always.

Lizzie imagined being in that yellow beach house with a man like Darryl Connelly, and it gave her a chill. Then she thought of leaving her sister there, completely and totally unattended. She'd never believed Connelly to be an actual danger, but the way he looked right now—the way he grit his teeth and narrowed his eyes—there was something not right about that expression.

She knew people, and there was something off about this one. There was something wrong with this man, something beyond having terrible taste in women and not paying attention to Jenna's games and planning to send her to boarding school. Connelly was cold, calculating, and his expression gave her the willies. No matter how unpleasant the thought, she couldn't chicken out and leave Jenna to deal with him alone.

"I'd love to stay with you, if you really don't mind," she said.

"Not at all." Connelly offered his hand to assist her to her feet. Lizzie sucked it up and took that hand.

It was surprisingly cold.

Chapter 15

Sam stared at the computer screen, unable to tear himself away even though he knew he had no business here. This late on a Saturday afternoon he should be at home, or maybe in a bar looking for a one-night woman who would make him forget the forever-woman who was firmly entrenched in his mind. At the very least he should be tailing an insurance fraud suspect or staking out the subject of a nasty child custody case. Instead he was in his office, trying to find out as much as he could about Lizzie's little sister.

If he found something new, he'd have an excuse to track Lizzie down so he could share the information.

What a putz he was. He shouldn't need any excuse for hunting down Lizzie except the truth—that he didn't want to let her go.

He'd been at it so long his mind was getting numb;

his thoughts often strayed from the words on the computer screen as he went back and back and around, gathering whatever information he could on Connelly and his stepdaughter and even the woman Connelly was engaged to marry. There wasn't much to be found where Heather was concerned. There was nothing new, nothing he hadn't found when he'd first investigated her. She came from money, but had none herself, unless you counted a hefty allowance. Daddy kept control of it all. Heather was an only child who'd surely been a disappointment to her parents, if what he'd found on her was any indication. Was it a coincidence that one day she'd likely come into a nice inheritance from her father? Likely not. Darryl Connelly apparently made a habit of marrying money.

Sam made himself call an end to the cyber investigation of Heather Mann. She was leading him nowhere. He went back again, and his search led him down a money trail, one he barely paid any mind to as he was distracted by thoughts of Lizzie and wherever the hell she might be. Jenna's mother had had money, inherited from her husband. Connelly had money, inherited from his first wife. What a sad couple they had been, leeches sucking those around them dry. Connelly was still a leech, and Heather was his next victim. Poor Jenna. Maybe Lizzie was right, and the girl needed a normal, loving family. He hadn't been able to find anything normal or loving about Connelly.

A series of numbers and paragraphs of legalese caught Sam's attention, as if they leaped off the page to speak to him. He quit ruminating about Lizzie and gave all his attention to what he'd found. This was public information, buried deep, but still—not exactly a secret if you knew where to look. Darryl Connelly had money, that was true, but he didn't have as much as one might think. He'd made bad investments, overbought—real estate and cars for the most part—and while he wasn't in the red, he was headed there. Fast.

The rest of the fortune, the money that kept Connelly in cars and blondes and beach property, was Jenna's.

A tingle of warning crept up Sam's spine as a possible scenario formed in his mind. Connelly finds out who Lizzie is and a warning bullet is fired into her house? He hadn't thought there was any reason for such a violent and scattered response, had quickly dismissed that theory when it had first occurred to him, but if Connelly believed that Lizzie was out to take Jenna and her fortune…would he do anything to keep things as they were? Anything at all? Were those stray shots just the beginning?

Sam used his office phone to try Lizzie's cell. Again. It immediately went to voice mail, which meant she had it turned off. He didn't bother to leave a message. What would he say? He called Mike's cell and got an answer. Too-loud music played in the background, indicating an early start to the weekend night's fun, so Sam raised his voice.

"Lizzie was talking to a woman at Jenna's soccer practice," he said without preamble. "Who was she?" It was a shot in the dark—but that was all he had.

Mike shouted into the phone. "I don't know. A pretty blonde with a redheaded kid on the soccer team. Lizzie never mentioned a name." He must've stepped outside, because suddenly the music was silenced.

"We have to find her. Get in here, now." Sam slammed the phone down without waiting for a response and dialed again. He didn't like the gnawing feeling that had settled in his gut.

Jenna chattered all through dinner, which consisted of hot dogs and hamburgers cooked on a tragically expensive grill that sat on the deck. There were chips and pickles and nice, soft buns. It was a simple but surprisingly tasty meal from a man who rarely had to fend for himself. The view from the deck was spectacular; the Gulf of Mexico at sunset.

Now and then Lizzie allowed a stray thought for Sam. She'd turned off her cell phone, knowing he might try to call and not wanting to have to deal with the choice to answer or ignore him. If he or any potential clients called, they could leave a message. She'd check those messages tomorrow, or in a day or two. She was on vacation, after all.

She and Jenna had plenty of time to talk. After Lizzie had returned from the hotel with her bags, Connelly had actually left the two girls there alone while he went to the grocery store. The conversation had continued much as it had on the beach. Food, shoes, Buffy... Connelly had taken his time; he'd been gone two hours. Two wonderful hours. He must trust her if he'd leave her with Jenna for so long. Maybe somehow this sister thing would work out, after all. She'd give a little; he'd give a little. Maybe somewhere in the middle there rested a decent compromise.

Lizzie picked at her hamburger, eating little since her stomach was in knots. Everything was going well, but she was excited. Too excited to eat, as if she were the little kid. Jenna ate well. Like most kids, a grilled hot dog was one of her favorite foods. Maybe Connelly knew that; maybe he wasn't the monster she wanted to believe him to be. Maybe he couldn't help that he sometimes came over like a creepy guy. He ate a hamburger and a hot dog and a bunch of chips, acting, for the most part, like a normal person. Huh.

It soon became clear that Jenna's most recent ramblings were not entirely without purpose. She praised first Lizzie and then Connelly; she mentioned that it was quite a coincidence that Lizzie and Homer were history and that Heather wasn't around; she suggested that the two adults take a walk on the beach after supper. Then she looked directly at Lizzie and waggled her eyebrows.

Great. Jenna was trying to play matchmaker, and she wasn't being very subtle about it. Knowing Heather would soon be a permanent member of the family was probably her motivation. Who wouldn't try to snag another stepmother, any other stepmother, when Heather was the only option on the table?

If there was ever a man Lizzie was *not* suited to, it was Darryl Connelly. She stared at him for a moment. Not that he'd ever consider it, but if she could make herself get romantically involved with Connelly, she'd be a part of Jenna's family without the drama of calling up old wounds. She could see her sister every day, keep her out of boarding school and make an absolute fool of herself at soccer games.

If she couldn't have Sam, what difference did it make who she ended up with?

Could she even stomach allowing Connelly to touch her?

Would he *want* to touch her? She really didn't think she was his type. At all. Maybe if she bleached her hair and got a boob job and donated a few brain cells to a worthy cause, he'd look at her twice, but even then, there was no guarantee.

Of course, he was looking at her now, smiling, appearing to be quite amused with the entire situation. He looked *so* amused, Lizzie was very glad her casual outfit for the evening was not nearly as revealing as her bikini had been. She thought of allowing Connelly to touch her in the way Sam had, and her insides turned cold. She suddenly felt a little sick to her stomach. Maybe she wasn't as tough as she'd always thought she was. Maybe she wasn't willing to do *anything*, after all.

"What do you say?" Connelly asked when it appeared everyone had finished their meal. "A walk on the beach?"

Lizzie considered the offer for a moment. "It wouldn't be right for us to go without Jenna."

"I don't mind," Jenna said, jumping out of her seat and gathering dirty plates. "I'll do the dishes while y'all walk. If you don't hurry you'll miss the prettiest part of the sunset. Go! Go!" she urged as she all but ran into the house and toward the sink with an armful of dirty plates.

Connelly raised his eyebrows, stood slowly and offered his hand to Lizzie. "She insists. We might as well not argue with her. My Jenna can be very stubborn when she sets her mind to a task."

Lizzie took his cold hand and rose to her feet. She wondered what Connelly would say when he had her alone. In spite of the smile on his face, it would likely not be pleasant. Still, she had come here knowing what she was getting herself into, and she might as well take her medicine. No matter how unpleasant it might be.

* * *

"I know it's illegal," Sam said calmly, not for the first time. "But this is important. I have to find the woman who's in possession of this cell phone. Now. You have the capability to ping that phone and find it." If Lizzie ever turned the freakin' cell on! He'd left her a half-dozen messages, for all the good it had done him.

Maybe Connelly was nothing but a money-grubbing sleaze, and there was no trouble at all. Sam had to wonder if he was making this more than it was so he'd have an excuse to track down Lizzie. Not knowing where she was or if she was safe was driving him nuts. He didn't lose control; he didn't let anything affect him this way. And yet, here he was.

The man on the other end of the line was maddening. "Has this chick been kidnapped? Is she a kidnapper? Is her life in danger? Is she wanted for some heinous crime and she's about to do whatever it is all over again?"

"She's missing. That's all I know."

"That's not enough reason to risk federal prison, man," the computer genius whined. The geek had been a wealth of information in the past, but he was playing it safe these days. Well, safer than usual. He was sure the feds were on his scent—and he might be right. "Why'd you call me, anyway? If this is legit you can call the cops, call the state troopers, call the cell phone company."

"That'll take too long." Sam had too much to do to continue to argue. He spit out Lizzie's cell phone number, hoping the man on the other end of the line would eventually come to his senses.

For a long moment he sat at his desk with his head in his hands, trying to convince himself that he was overreacting. So, Connelly was almost out of money, and his stepdaughter had more than enough for everyone. That didn't make him a monster, just unlucky. Maybe he'd fired into Lizzie's house—maybe not. It wasn't as if she'd gone missing. Hell, she'd left town on her own, to get away from him. Everything could be explained away logically—so why was his stomach in knots?

Once again, he tried to call Lizzie, and when he immediately got the same message about the customer being unavailable, he cursed at the disembodied voice.

The stroll on the beach might appear to be romantic to anyone watching, even though Lizzie and Connelly didn't hold hands or lean into one another, the way lovers might.

"You confuse me," Connelly said, his eyes on the lapping waves that were just a few feet away. "I thought for sure you'd come around to stir up trouble, but you haven't said a word to Jenna about your claims and you turned down my offer of money. So, tell me the truth. What do you want?"

"I want to know her," Lizzie said. "I want her in my life, just as a friend if that's all I can have. I don't want to disrupt her life."

He sighed as if in relief. "She's too young to be told that she's not who she believes herself to be. Maybe when she's older…"

"Exactly!" Lizzie said. "In a few years we could break the news to her and maybe by then, if she knows me and we get along as well as I think we will, she'll be glad."

"I suppose," Connelly said, less than enthusiastically. "We'll cross that bridge when we come to it."

Time to get tough. He'd asked what she wanted; she'd gladly tell him. "Promise me you won't send her to boarding school," Lizzie said. "That's all I ask. That's all I want, for now."

Connelly looked uncertain. He squinted and his lips narrowed. "I promised Heather…"

"Screw Heather," Lizzie interrupted. "If you marry a man with kids then you deal with having them in the house and in your life."

He looked less than certain. "I could lose Heather over this."

"Better than losing Jenna, if you ask me."

"Maybe you're right," Connelly said, oddly accepting. "Heather can be very demanding, and it's starting to wear thin."

They came to a sort of pact as they walked on the beach and watched the sun set. She could spend time with Jenna, as much time as she wished. They wouldn't tell the child the truth of her parentage, not for many years. Lizzie couldn't imagine a romantic relationship with Connelly, but she disliked him less near the end of the walk than she had when they'd set out. Maybe he wasn't a complete ass after all. The jury was still out on that one.

After the surprisingly pleasant stroll on the beach, Lizzie and Jenna sat on the well-lit deck, while an unexpectedly competent Darryl Connelly made homemade ice cream, even though he couldn't enjoy any of it himself thanks to his lactose intolerance—which was really more information than she needed. Still, Lizzie would definitely consider it a sacrifice if she had to make ice cream she couldn't eat. No wonder Connelly was so often a grump. He made ice cream and couldn't have even a bite.

Chocolate ice cream, at that. Maybe his lactose intolerance was part of the reason for his sour mood. No ice cream, no cheese, no milk on his cereal. No banana splits.

The two girls ate huge bowls of ice cream, they laughed, they talked more about movies and television shows and books, agreeing more often than not. It was like a dream. A really, really good dream. Jenna liked her; Lizzie was certain of it. The truth wouldn't be such a shock, when it finally came out, if they truly liked one another, if they were friends.

When Jenna began to yawn, she fought her obvious weariness. It was a losing battle at the end of a long day. Connelly laughed at Jenna's yawning and drooping eyes and sent the girl to bed. Lizzie planned to be close behind, but Connelly stopped her, saying he'd like to talk.

Lizzie was anxious to get to the guest room she'd been shown earlier, which was larger than her master bedroom at home and had a private bath. It was tastefully decorated, beach appropriate but not garishly so. She needed a long shower and a good night's sleep. Would she be able to sleep at all with Jenna—and Connelly—right down the hall? She was going to try. At the moment she felt as if she could sleep very well; she stifled a yawn of her own.

But Jenna had smiled over her shoulder upon hearing Connelly's invitation, so in order to give the girl a moment of happiness, Lizzie agreed.

He offered her a drink, expounding on his barkeeping skills as he offered her a margarita, a daiquiri or a cosmo. She passed, without telling him that she really didn't drink, then she asked for one of the caffeine-free diet sodas she'd seen in the fridge. He raised an eyebrow. So, she was dull. She didn't care what Connelly thought of her. Well, not much. He could make things so much easier where Jenna was concerned, if she played her cards right.

She sat on the deck and looked out over the moonlit water, remembering her fabulous day with Jenna, replaying every word of their conversations, picturing every lovely smile, hearing again the bell-like laugh. She had a sister. Her life wasn't a complete mess after all.

Too soon Connelly returned with her soda in a tall glass of ice, as well as a drink for himself. Looked like Scotch, maybe, but she was no expert. Both glasses were heavy crystal—naturally. She would've been happy with a cold can or a paper cup, but that wasn't Connelly's style. He sipped his drink slowly, while Lizzie took a long, refreshing swig of her soda.

He sat facing her, claiming the same chair where a little while ago Jenna had sat. Instead of a pleasant laugh and a girlish smile, he offered a serious expression that did nothing to lighten the mood. Heaven above, there was no way she could consider being romantically involved with a man like this one. They'd have to find another way for her to stay in Jenna's life.

"You're a lot of trouble," he said, then took another sip of his drink.

He said it with a hint of humor, so Lizzie laughed. "So I've been told."

"I must be honest. In the last days of Monica's life she was in a mood for confessing. I've known for years that Aldridge wasn't Jenna's biological father."

Lizzie cast a quick glance at the French doors, which

were cracked open very slightly. She didn't want Jenna learning the truth by overhearing a conversation. How traumatic that would be!

"Don't worry. Jenna sleeps like the dead," Connelly said, and then he grinned. The grin didn't last long. "Yes, Monica spilled the beans on her deathbed, so to speak, but she didn't tell me that Charlie Porter had a nosy daughter. I assumed he and those connected to him were completely out of the picture. I wasn't even sure he knew about the kid until you arrived on the scene. I did some searching online and connected you two. You showing up the way you did couldn't be a co-incidence."

Lizzie took another long swig of her soda and looked out over the beach. A couple walked in the surf, holding hands, whispering. The way they kept their heads together and stayed so close, it reminded her of Sam, even though he wasn't exactly the romantic type who'd be interested in strolls on the beach. Connelly glared at the couple. Judging by the expression on his face, he really did wish he owned the entire Orange Beach! What a loser.

"Charlie always cared about Jenna," Lizzie said, surprised that her words were slightly slurred. She must be more exhausted than she'd realized. "If he hadn't believed she was well cared for, you would've met him a long time ago."

"And yet that is not enough for you," Connelly said in a low voice.

"I had to see for myself." Lizzie closed her eyes, just for a moment. "I had to know her. I wish I could be sure…"

Suddenly Connelly was there, supporting the hand that loosely gripped a half-empty and suddenly heavy crystal glass of soda. Had she dozed off? How embarrassing. "You're tired," he said, sounding almost caring. Almost. "Finish your soda and get to bed. We'll talk about this later."

Lizzie looked at the soda, brown and bubbly. If she finished it all, she'd probably have to get up in the middle of the night to pee. She wanted to sleep for hours, uninterrupted. But when Connelly raised the glass to her lips, she drank. Drinking was easier than arguing with him.

Maybe if she hadn't been so tired she would've been alarmed by the way he made her drink, but it was easier to let him do as he wished. The cold, bubbly liquid poured down her throat. Her eyes fluttered. Darkness descended.

She didn't make it to bed.

Danny and Mike met Sam at the office, each of them contributing their own pieces of information. Mike had tracked down the woman and child he'd seen with Lizzie at the park. There were only two redheads on Jenna's team, so the search had not been a difficult one. Mike had introduced himself, given them a very official-looking business card and asked them to repeat every word of the conversation with Lizzie and Jenna. The mother had taken some convincing, but Mike had done the job.

Jackpot. If Jenna was headed for Orange Beach, so was Lizzie. Sam felt a wave of relief. At least he knew which direction to drive when he got in his car!

Danny had tracked down Heather, who was pouting because her fiancé had told her not to join him on the trip to the beach. He needed some time alone with his stepdaughter, he'd said. She was unhappy with Connelly, she was feeling neglected, and when Danny had found her she'd been making her displeasure evident by hanging all over some other guy's neck in a trendy bar in downtown Birmingham. Danny wasn't entirely positive, since the lights had been dim and the place had been crowded, but it appeared that Heather had also had her hand down the guy's pants.

Sam didn't like this at all. Why would Connelly tell his fiancée to stay home, when he was so obviously smitten with her? He tried Lizzie's phone again. It still went directly to voice mail.

"Get Curtis and follow me," Sam said as he stalked out of the office, headed for his car. He had the address of Connelly's beach house, and a bad feeling to go along with it. If he found Connelly and Jenna there enjoying an innocent family vacation, he'd still want to find Lizzie—but maybe the gnawing in his gut would subside.

"I need to get my gun," Mike said. "Wait a couple of minutes and I'll—"

"No." He wasn't waiting a minute longer to get on the road, much less two. He hoped to be wrong, but he didn't think he'd find anything innocent about Darryl Connelly.

"I'm driving. We'll be five minutes behind you," Danny said as Sam opened his car door and slipped inside.

Sam halfheartedly nodded his head. Considering his mood, it was entirely possible five minutes was all he'd need.

Lizzie slept deeply—very deeply—and then fell into the most bizarre dream. The colors were amazing; it was the most vivid dream she'd ever had. Her dad was there. Sam was there and so was Jenna. Amy, her best friend from Mobile, and Carrie, who remained a friend even though her days and nights were now filled with a husband and a new baby. She should make a point to see them more often, even though their lives had taken different directions.

In the dream the people she loved were all around her, and she felt better than she ever had. Not at all alone, not at all odd or different or lost.

She loved; she was loved.

Lizzie woke slowly, drowsily, to realize that she wasn't sleeping in the soft bed Jenna had shown her to earlier in the day, but was sitting in a hard deck chair, with Darryl Connelly leaning over her. She went from a good dream to a nightmare, in less than a heartbeat.

It was a struggle to keep her eyes open. They drifted closed, and she forced them open again. It was dark out here; she could barely see Connelly. The lights inside the house were off, so there was nothing but moonlight to illuminate the night. The man who was too close to her smiled. He looked quite pleased with himself. Her heart thumped. Oh, no. Had he decided he liked the idea of Jenna's matchmaking?

His hand drifted toward her face, and when she tried to raise her hand to swat him away she found it was too difficult. Her entire body was heavy, her vision swam. Connelly's palm came to rest firmly over her mouth. "This is all your fault. I want you to remember that," he whispered. "I could've waited. I might've found a way to gradually transfer the funds into my own accounts, but no, you had to show up with your sister act and put it all in jeopardy."

"I don't know what you're talking about," Lizzie tried to say, her sounds muffled against Connelly's palm.

Somehow, he understood her. "Don't you? Surely you realize that the bulk of the family fortune is Jenna's, not mine."

Lizzie's eyes widened. Well, didn't that change everything... "I didn't know," she whispered.

Connelly leaned over, placing his face close to hers. "No one knows you're here, Miss Porter. You checked out of the hotel and came here without telling a soul. Maybe someone saw us on the beach earlier, but it was a friendly conversation."

She tried to fight but couldn't. In fact, she could barely move. "What have you done?"

"A date-rape drug in your soda," he explained. "Not that I plan to rape you. That would be despicable. But the young man I bought it from assured me that the lady who consumed the drug would be unable to fight, practically unable to move at all." He slowly moved his hand away from her mouth. "I wonder if you can scream. I doubt it, but this is new territory for me. I had to wait longer than I had planned, thanks to that annoying couple on the beach. I had to wait until I knew the coast was clear."

With his hand away from her mouth, Lizzie tried to shout, to warn Jenna, to raise an alarm with the neighbors—who were much too far away. All she needed was to make enough noise to wake Jenna. The child had to run, to get out of the house and away from Connelly *now!* The noise she made was not much more than a whisper. She didn't have the strength to scream.

Connelly was apparently relieved. He even gave her a smile. "You wanted a relationship with your little sister, and now you're going to have one. The two of you are going to die together, and in Monday morning papers all over the country the story will run. Night Swimming Gone Wrong. Painter and Young Girl Drown. Once the autopsies are done I suppose it's possible they'll discover that you two were related, and I will appear to be suitably shocked at the news."

"Don't hurt her," Lizzie said, her voice slurred even though Connelly no longer held a hand to her mouth. "She doesn't know anything. It doesn't matter anymore. Just…kill me and leave her alone."

His eyebrows arched. "How noble of you. However, since you have presented me with a permanent solution to my problem, I'd be a fool not to take advantage of the opportunity. Come along, sweetheart," he said sweetly. "You and your sister are going for a little swim."

Chapter 16

Sam flew down the interstate, and didn't lower his speed much when he left the main highway and hit the winding two-lane road. He drove on automatic, his reflexes sharp but his mind elsewhere. If anything happened to Lizzie, he didn't know what he'd do. How could he live with himself when he'd all but pushed her away, driving her to desperation, making her face a man like Darryl Connelly on her own?

For once he prayed to be wrong. He prayed Lizzie was far away from Orange Beach, maybe visiting a friend or holed up in a nice hotel room or simply putting as many miles as possible between her and him. He prayed Connelly was greedy but not violent, a leech but a harmless leech. He hadn't told his girlfriend to stay home this week because he had plans to hurt Jenna, but because he was second-guessing his decision to get involved with someone so shallow.

For years Sam had blamed Dottie Ann for their failed marriage, but deep down he also blamed himself. He'd chosen her, after all. He'd picked her as his wife, not looking any deeper than the beauty that hadn't lasted and the smile she'd always worn for him, in those early days.

Since then he'd been afraid to even consider choosing again; he'd been terrified of making the same mistake all over again. He could fix everyone else's problems, but his own were irreparable. A part of him was broken, apparently, so he'd shut it down, living a safe lonely life and convincing himself that was what he wanted. No ties. No commitment. No life-altering mistakes.

And now there was Lizzie, who said what was on her mind, who gave her whole heart along with her body, who loved him in a way no one else ever had—or ever would.

He loved her back. He wanted to keep her in his life. And when the time had come for him to tell her so, he'd chickened out and remained silent, leaving her floundering. Breaking her heart.

The trees that lined the road flew past, and beyond the car the world here was dark. His headlights illuminated the deserted road ahead, a road that seemed to roll ahead of him without end.

Lucky for her, if she could count anything "lucky" tonight, Connelly wasn't in the best shape. Getting an uncooperative and heavy-limbed Lizzie out of her chair, across the deck and down the stairs onto the sand was difficult for him and took more time than he'd planned, or so she deduced from his muttering foul language. Since she could barely feel her own body, much less move, she couldn't even protect herself as she was dragged and dropped and mishandled. She was limp, useless, as he moved her.

She'd be bruised tomorrow, thanks to the way he banged her body around. Oh, wait, no, she wouldn't be bruised at all. She'd be dead.

Breathless and sweating, Connelly finally dumped her on the sand before going back up the deck stairs and into the house.

For Jenna.

There was an almost full moon in the early-morning sky, so she wasn't lost in complete darkness. Moving was difficult, bordering on impossible, but still, Lizzie rotated her head and surveyed the area. A few feet away her purse and small overnight bag sat. Was Connelly going to throw them in the ocean with her? Put them in her truck and make it look as though she'd never been invited to stay here? Had he removed all signs of her from the cottage where she'd been so happy for such a short period of time? She didn't know what he might be thinking, but the sight of her purse lying in the sand gave her hope.

Had he bothered to search it, or did he think she didn't carry anything but lipstick and money in her purse, like most women? Thanking her stars that she wasn't like most women, Lizzie crawled toward her purse. Every inch she moved was an effort, but she thought of Jenna, twelve years old and ignorant of so much. Poor Jenna was unaware that she had a sister, and that her stepfather was a money-hungry psychopath.

Her body wanted to lie there, uncooperative and heavy and pathetic. Her mind fought, knowing it was the only chance she and Jenna had. Lizzie reached out, dug her fingers into the sand, tensed every muscle in her body as best she could, and pulled herself toward the bag. The difficult movement took her an inch or so forward, which wasn't much—but was more than she'd thought herself capable of a few seconds ago. Connelly had complained about having to wait. Was it possible the drug would wear off before he had a chance to kill her? She blinked hard, reached out again and pulled her body through the sand. Pain she could handle, but there wasn't any pain. Her body was horribly weak, numbed and heavy. It was almost as if she were dragging someone else's body through the sand.

But she continued to move forward, an inch at a time, toward her things.

Finally, she reached out and touched her bag. She slipped her hand into her purse, searching for her Taser. Her hand fumbled around, finding a small first-aid kit, a change purse, a pack of gum, and her cell phone. No Taser. Crap. She grabbed the cell phone, intent on calling Sam. He wouldn't get here in time, but she could tell him what was happening, and that she loved him, even if he was a thick-headed commitmentphobe.

Since she was about to die, maybe she'd leave that last part out.

With trembling hands she turned on the phone. It took a moment for the cell to boot up, and then she waited while the screen indicated that it was searching for a signal. Searching, searching…

Connelly ran down the stairs, his feet thumping, his mumbled words less than kind. When he came around the corner Lizzie saw an unconscious Jenna draped over his shoulder. Apparently the smaller girl was much easier to handle than Lizzie had been.

Once on the sand he roughly placed Jenna down and ran toward Lizzie, kicking the cell phone out of her hand. Her hand stung at the blow, the cell phone flew, landing in the sand several feet away. It might as well be a hundred miles.

"You shouldn't be able to move," he said as he dropped beside her, balanced on his haunches, smiling, still. "I'd hunt that incompetent drug dealer down and kill him when I was done here, if I hadn't already taken care of that loose end this afternoon, shortly after I purchased the drugs. He didn't see it coming. Apparently I don't look at all dangerous, which worked to my advantage. Were you by chance looking for this?" He pulled her Taser from behind his back, as if it had been tucked in a back pocket or in his waistband. "I was so surprised to find this in your purse."

Was it her imagination, or was a touch of control returning to her body? Her hand hurt where he'd kicked her. She wasn't quite as heavy as she'd been when she'd first come to and seen Connelly leaning over her. "You can have the money," she said. Would he notice that her voice was not quite as slurred as it had been a few minutes ago? "Let me take Jenna and go. You'll never see or hear from us again, I swear."

"Yeah, like I believe that," Connelly muttered. He moved behind her and lifted her into a sitting position once more.

"No," Lizzie whispered, and she found that the drug he'd given her did not take away her ability to cry. Tears ran down her cheeks; her chest rumbled with sorrow and regret. If she hadn't stuck her nose where it didn't belong, if she'd left Jenna alone, her sister's worst problems would be boarding school and an embezzling stepfather. Neither was exactly nice; neither was fatal.

Lizzie gathered all her strength and jerked her arms to the side, just as Connelly started to lift her.

An angry Connelly cursed as he pushed Lizzie to the ground. He grabbed her arm and dragged her toward the water.

Lizzie didn't have any fight left in her. The sand he dragged her through scraped and burned, and it felt as if Connelly was trying to pull her arm out of its socket, and yet she couldn't move. "Run, Jenna!" What had been meant to be a scream came out as not much more than a whisper. Lying on the sand closer to the house, Jenna didn't move.

She felt the soft, dry sand beneath her grow hard as they moved onto the packed, wet sand where gentle gulf waves had lapped. Then they reached the water, which was surprisingly cold. Lizzie gasped at the shock, and still she could barely move. The waves danced around her, soaking her clothes. Lizzie gasped again as Connelly pulled her deeper into the gulf and the cold salty water slapped her face, dribbling up her nose. She flailed without purchase. In the deeper water she'd have no chance of digging in and holding her ground; she'd have no chance of saving herself so she could save Jenna. As unpleasant as it was, the chill of the water seemed to invigorate her, a little, to wake her up, to bring her strength closer to the surface.

Her head broke the water, and she fought for air, gasping hard. Connelly pushed her head beneath the water again, but she twisted her head to the side and once again was able to take in air. She fought upward and looked toward Jenna, and her eyes went beyond the too-still girl. On the street just beyond the house a car's lights broke the darkness of night. It stopped. A car door slammed. And Lizzie gathered every ounce of strength she could find to scream.

And then with a strong push from Connelly, the water took her again.

Sam's eyes were on the beach house. A couple of lights burned inside. Not that he would've hesitated to knock on the door even if all the lights had been out. He was headed for the front door at a run when he heard it.

The sound that claimed his attention was weak and distant, and it did not come from the house before him. It came from the beach.

Sam ran alongside the house, toward the gulf waters and the sound. Human? Maybe. He couldn't be sure. He didn't know if Lizzie was here or not; he didn't know why Connelly had planned to be here without any witnesses, not even his fiancée, but he didn't like any of this. And his instincts had been in overdrive since he'd found out that so much of the family fortune was actually Jenna's and that Connelly had taken pains to make sure that he and Jenna were here alone this week.

In the moonlight, he saw Connelly walking away from the gulf and toward the small body on the sand. In an instant he took it all in. An unconscious Jenna, breathing but unaware; a Taser lying in the sand; Lizzie's huge purse, the contents spilling out.

Sam drew his semiautomatic, thumbed off the safety and took aim at Connelly as the man approached Jenna. Only at that moment did Connelly realize that he wasn't alone. He stopped. His hands rose slowly. "You wouldn't shoot an unarmed man, would you?"

"Give me a reason," Sam said calmly. "Where's Lizzie?"

"Who?"

Sam ratcheted the slide. The sharp noise the movement made was crisp in the night—and an unmistakable warning. His hands remained steady as Connelly took a step back toward the water.

"Oh, her," Connelly said. "She was here but she left." He licked his lips. "She has some crazy notion about Jenna…"

"They're sisters, and I suspect you know that." Sam took a step, following Connelly toward the water. Behind the man there was a splash, a panting noise, and a dimly lit head barely lifted out of the water. He couldn't see well, but he knew who was out there.

Lizzie, struggling. Sam's hands began to shake.

Connelly took advantage of the distraction and turned, running away from Sam, toward the water. He ran into the surf, splashing and fighting the waves and reached for Lizzie. He grabbed her hair and held her head above water. Barely. "Throw the gun away."

Sam didn't obey the order. He stood his ground, and Connelly responded by pushing Lizzie's head under the surface. He held her there, even as she struggled weakly.

"Now," Connelly said calmly, pushing Lizzie's head down an inch more.

Lizzie was too close to Connelly, and there were too many dark shadows surrounding them. Tempted as Sam was to end this here and now, any shot would be uncertain, a risk he didn't dare to take. Sam tossed the gun aside, and Connelly yanked on Lizzie's hair and pulled her face from the gulf waters. She gasped, fought for a breath and coughed. Her hair fell over her face, stuck to her skin. Once her head was above water, she barely moved at all. She looked as if she'd sink for good if Connelly let her go.

"No one's been hurt here tonight," Sam said, trying to keep his voice calm while inside he was on fire, panicking in a way he never had before. "Let's get Lizzie out of the water and talk about this. We can all get what we want from this without the situation getting out of hand."

"I want it all," Connelly said. "How is that going to work?"

"Do you really want Jenna?" Sam asked sharply. "I promise you, that's all Lizzie cares about. Not the money, not the house. I can have a lawyer friend draw up the papers before noon, if that's what you want. You let Lizzie have visitation rights, the money is all yours."

"It's not that easy."

Sam took a step toward the shore, and Connelly responded by once again pushing Lizzie's head beneath the water. This time she didn't even have the strength to struggle. She just lay there, drowning.

"Okay." He backed up a step, and Connelly immediately yanked Lizzie's head up.

Sam tried to think clearly, which seemed almost impossible as he stood on the sand, helpless. The guys should be here soon, unless they'd been foolish enough to drive the speed limit. He didn't think they would, especially if Danny was at the wheel. How would Connelly react when he was outnumbered? Not well, Sam imagined. He'd have to be ready to move, when he heard Danny's car.

What if they thought he'd overreacted in racing here? What if his most trusted employees were headed here at a snail's pace because they thought there was nothing to find but a disenchanted ex-girlfriend? Unlikely, but certainly not impossible.

Time. He needed time.

"Did you take a potshot at Lizzie's house?"

Connelly grimaced. "Considering my position I don't think it'll make things any worse to admit to that mistake. I was drunk and angry that night, I didn't know how to handle the situation. If I had to do it again I'd plan better. I'd shoot the interfering bitch between the eyes and burn her house down."

"No one's dead yet. There are better ways to do this," Sam said once again, pushing down the panic and anger that threatened to chase away all reason. "Ways that don't call for murder. Murder always catches up with a man. I've seen it happen time and again. You might get away with it for a while, but there's always someone checking out the facts, examining the details, and somehow, someway, this will all head back to you. There's a money trail. Don't think the cops won't suspect you right out of the gate. Then there's me. I'm a witness, Connelly. Right now I'm only a witness to attempted murder, but if Lizzie stops breathing, if she dies, what are you going to do about me? I'm not drugged senseless. I don't weigh fifty to a hundred pounds less than you do, the way these girls do. I will fight back, be assured of that fact."

Connelly lost his confident glare, but he didn't push Lizzie's head into the dark gulf waters again.

"All the money in the world won't do you any good when you're in prison."

There it was, the rumble of an engine on the street. Betting that it was Danny and the others, not really caring if it was or not, Sam rushed forward. He'd held back as long as he could.

He ran, through the sand, into the water. Connelly was slow to react, and Sam was there as the man tried to once again force Lizzie under the water.

Sam reached for Lizzie and delivered a blow to Connelly's jaw at the same time. His fist had less power than it would've if he'd put his entire body behind it, but he wouldn't leave Lizzie in that man's hands a half second longer than he had to, and he wasn't about to let her fall back into the water. Connelly released her, Sam caught her in his arms and the coward who had tried to kill her ran for the shore…where he was met by three armed and angry men.

Even Connelly wasn't stupid enough to take them all on.

Curtis twisted Connelly's arm behind his back and held him in a painful and precarious position. All three men watched solemnly as Sam carried a limp Lizzie out of the gulf. "Call 911."

"Already done," Mike said.

Danny ran back up the beach, headed for Jenna. The girl was stirring, but still out of it.

"What did you give them?" Sam asked, holding on to Lizzie as tightly as he could. She hadn't stirred; she was so damn cold.

Connelly didn't answer immediately, but Curtis gave his arm a twist that made him scream. "Sleeping pills in the ice cream," he confessed. "Not enough to kill them, just enough to knock them out."

"What else?"

For a moment Connelly didn't answer, then Curtis gave his arm another small twist that got results. "That's all I gave Jenna. The other one I gave a drug to make her senseless, something that won't stay in her system long. Some kind of party drug that won't show up after she's…" He choked on his words.

"After she's dead," Sam said, his voice surprisingly cold.

Lizzie breathed, but not as strongly as he'd like. Her heart beat in an unsteady rhythm, and she lay limp against him. If she died… His insides churned and grew heavy. That was not a thought he could deal with, not now, not ever.

Sam glared at the pathetic man and delivered a warning. A promise. "If she dies, I'll kill you with my bare hands."

In the distance sirens wailed, and Sam dropped to the sand with Lizzie in his arms.

Chapter 17

Something beeped, and then again. And again. How annoying. Lizzie started to open her eyes, but the lights were too bright so she pressed them shut again. Her mind was spinning as she tried to piece together where she was, what had happened. Connelly. Water.

"Jenna," she croaked.

A warm hand wrapped around hers, and a comforting, deep voice said, "Jenna's fine."

Lizzie forced her eyes open. Sam? What was he doing here, rumpled and damp and paler than she'd ever seen him? "You swear." Her throat burned, but she continued. "You swear to me that she's all right."

Sam's wan smile reassured her. "I swear. They insisted on putting her in the pediatric ward, or I'd have you both in the same room. She woke up, called me Homer and went back to sleep. Danny and Mike are taking turns sitting with her." His smile faded. "She has no idea what happened."

"Connelly?"

"In jail. By the time we're done with him he'll be going away for a long time."

"Good." She really should take her hand from his, but she was so weak it would be more of an effort than she wanted to exert. Besides, she liked the feeling, even if it wouldn't last.

Somehow she'd get custody of Jenna, and she'd make everything right. She'd dedicate herself to the child, love her, make sure she knew every day that she was loved. Both of them were in desperate need of a family, even if that family consisted of two sisters who barely knew one another.

Maybe together they could learn how to cook. Neither of them had had a mother around to teach them, so it just seemed right. They could shop for clothes. And shoes. They'd go to the movies. All in good time.

"I want to sit with her," Lizzie insisted. "She doesn't even know Danny and Mike!"

"I introduced them. They charmed her, and you're not going anywhere until you build up some strength. You collapsing on the floor of Jenna's hospital room won't make this night any better for her."

True enough. Lizzie let her eyes drift closed. The light really was too harsh here.

"Lizzie, I…" Sam began, and she could hear in his voice where he was going. At the moment he was filled with pain, sorrow and regret. She'd seen all that in his eyes, and more.

"Stop," she said softly, her eyes remaining closed. She felt as though she was sinking into the hard mattress, melting toward sleep—or unconsciousness. There wasn't much time to say what had to be said before sleep claimed her once more. "I have an idea of what you're going to say, but…not now. Not here. We'll have time to talk after we get home and I'm myself again. You're freaked out, at the moment," she said.

"Damn right," he muttered.

Besides, she was bruised and loopy and wearing a completely unflattering hospital gown—not that she'd ever cared much about her clothes. "Wait," she whispered, and then she went silent, finding speech to be more difficult. "Just wait." She wanted him to be sure before he said another word. She didn't want bedside confessions that might not stand up to the drama of everyday life.

When Sam climbed into the hospital bed with her sometime later, stretching his body close to hers on the narrow mattress, she smiled. His arms went carefully around her. He was no longer damp, but felt warm and dry. Having him there made her feel stronger. Better. More complete.

At some point a nurse tried to make him leave. He refused.

She dreamed of drowning and panicked. She woke to a soothing deep voice in her ear and warm, strong arms that held her close. After that, her dreams were more pleasant. She was safe here.

When she woke again, Sam was gone. Her heart sank. Didn't that just figure? She'd known he'd recover from his emotional upset and come to his senses sooner or later; she just hadn't figured it would be quite so soon. Mike sat in a chair by the door, and he smiled at her when he realized she was awake.

"About time," he said.

"Jenna?"

He nodded his head. "She's doing good. Right now she thinks the two of you got a really bad case of food poisoning. She knows her stepfather is in trouble with the law and that's why he's not here, but no one's explained to her exactly what that trouble is, until now. Sam's talking to her."

Lizzie struggled to sit up, and Mike all but vaulted toward the bed.

"I have to be there when she finds out. She's twelve! This is going to be traumatic, and she'll need all the support she can get."

Mike put a strong hand on her shoulder. "You need to stay right here."

She looked the big man in the eye. "Who's going to stop me? You?"

He was wise enough to recognize that he didn't have even the smallest chance of keeping her from Jenna.

Jenna sat up in the bed, looking much better than Lizzie had when he'd left her. The young girl had been drugged, too, but with sleeping pills instead of a potentially deadly combination of sleeping pills and a date-rape drug. And thank goodness she hadn't had to fight for her life in the ocean the way her big sister had.

"Sam is a much better name than Homer," she said brightly. "Was that Lizzie's idea of a joke?"

"Yep."

"She's so funny. Are you sure she's okay? I wish she was here. I'll feel better when I can see her."

"I know she'll be here as soon as she's able," Sam said honestly. "Now, there's something I have to tell you, and it's not very pleasant, but you need to know because it'll be in the papers and on the news, and the police are going to want to talk to you."

"About Darryl being in trouble?"

"Yes," Sam said. He explained as succinctly as he could that Darryl had been taking money from her trust fund, and that he was a greedy man who wanted it all, at any cost. His heart hurt when he told her that Darryl had tried to kill Lizzie. He didn't think it necessary to tell the kid that her stepfather would've killed her, too, if he'd had his way. She was a smart kid who would figure it out soon enough.

He also didn't tell Jenna that he was pretty sure Connelly had planned to kill her this week, Lizzie or no Lizzie. The sleeping pills were his own prescription, and he'd had much more than he needed with him. No wonder he'd made Heather stay home; he didn't want any witnesses. Yes, it was very possible that Connelly had planned all along to drug Jenna and put her in the ocean. If that was the case, Lizzie had just been a bonus.

Jenna wrinkled her nose. "I always knew Darryl was a freak for money, but why would he hurt Lizzie? That doesn't make any sense at all."

Sam opened his mouth to respond, but he was interrupted by a soft voice behind him.

"Because I'm your sister."

Sam jumped to his feet and turned around. Lizzie stood in the doorway, still looking like a drowned rat, wearing an ill-fitting hospital gown, leaning on Mike as if she couldn't stand without his support. She took his breath away.

Jenna looked confused as Mike walked Lizzie into the room and helped her to the side of the bed, where she sat. She reached out and took Jenna's hand. "I'm not sure how to tell you this in a way that doesn't hurt, but Harold Aldridge was not your biological father."

Jenna blinked twice. "I know. Mom told me before she died. She was on some drugs and one night she got weird and spilled the beans. Some guy named Charlie was my real father, she said, and then she told me that was a big secret and I could never tell anyone. Then she told me he was permanently out of the picture, so I figured he was dead. Is he… Is Charlie your father, too?"

Lizzie smiled. "Yes. Charlie Porter. You have his eyes." She lay down beside Jenna, much as Sam had lain with her last night. Both the girls relaxed. "There's more, but it can wait. The important thing is that you're my sister. We're family. I'm going to take good care of you, Jenna."

"This is just too weird," Jenna said, and then in spite of everything that had happened she smiled softly. "A sister! I always wanted a sister."

"Fair warning, I'm going to be a bossy big sister, on occasion. As soon as we're able, we're going to have a long talk about common sense and self-preservation," Lizzie said, attempting to sound stern. "I showed up at your soccer practice and at the beach, and you weren't the least bit suspicious?"

Jenna sighed long and dramatically. "I thought you were on the prowl for Darryl and were trying to get to him through me. In a weird way, it was romantic, I thought."

Lizzie's response was a tired scoff.

"It was wishful thinking, I suppose," Jenna said. "You're *so* much better than Heather."

Ten minutes later they were both asleep. Sam shooed

Mike out of the room and sat beside the bed. Lizzie had what she'd come to him for. She had a family— her sister. It had been a rough road, but all would be well. Now that she had this new responsibility, did she still want him in her life? Or had he done all that she required of him?

Lizzie stepped into her role as sister and guardian quite easily. The mansion Jenna had once lived in was Darryl's, and it was up for sale. He needed the money for his lawyers. For the moment, Lizzie and Jenna lived in Charlie's old house, but they'd been looking for something new, something suitable for a fresh start. They wanted a nice place that fell somewhere between a mansion and a starter home. Lizzie was able to work around Jenna's schedule, painting while her sister was in school or at soccer practice, which would soon be done for the season, taking weekends off, making a fool of herself at soccer games. Jenna sometimes rolled her eyes at Lizzie's rabid-fan behavior, but it was evident she was also pleased to have someone there who cared so much.

Lizzie wanted to make sure Jenna always knew she didn't care about the money her mother had left to her. She'd made arrangements to see that enough would be available for Jenna to continue to go to her expensive school, but beyond that, Lizzie planned to pay for everything. It wouldn't hurt Jenna to shop clearance sales once in a while and eat mac and cheese on occasion. One day she'd be filthy rich again, but that money was *hers,* and Lizzie wouldn't take a dime of it.

They didn't have to worry about Darryl Connelly anymore. If the only charges against him had been attempted murder and embezzlement, he could've made bond and been on the streets, awaiting trial. But thanks to his confession about killing the drug dealer who'd sold him the nasty stuff he'd rendered Lizzie senseless with, and thanks to a handful of dedicated police officers who put the case together very quickly, Darryl wasn't getting out of jail. Ever. And to think, she'd been grateful that he'd left her alone with Jenna for a couple of hours. He'd been out buying drugs to facilitate her murder! What a creep.

Lizzie even took a bit of pleasure in knowing that *all* his money was going to lawyers, for all the good it was going to do him.

Having Jenna in her life made her look at a lot of things differently. Just last week, Lizzie had made a call to her mother. The call had been more pleasant than she'd expected it to be, and they'd made plans to meet for a few days during the summer, while Jenna was out of school. Lizzie didn't expect she and her mother would ever be close— their relationship would never be ideal. But she wasn't going to push her mother away because that was easier than taking a chance.

This was an odd night. One of Jenna's friends from the soccer team had called to ask if Jenna could go to a movie and then back to her house for pizza. Jenna had seemed pleased and anxious to go, so Lizzie had driven her sister to the girl's house, said hello to the mother— Rebecca, the blonde she'd spoken to several weeks ago during a soccer practice—and then she'd headed home.

Her life was so much better than it had been. She was wonderfully content most of the time, but something was still missing. She knew too well what that "something" was, and the worries and heartache rose up most sharply in quiet moments like this one. Maybe one day they'd fade. Maybe not.

Lizzie collapsed on the couch, both lost in and terrified by the silence of the house. She hadn't realized how much noise a twelve-year-old could create until she'd lived with one for a few weeks. There was always conversation, phone calls, music playing in the background, television…constant sensory overload. The silence was so nice, she'd almost fallen asleep when the doorbell rang.

A neighbor, most likely, or maybe a real estate agent wanting to show the house. They were supposed to call first, but didn't always. She looked around the room and deemed it suitable, smoothed her hair and hurried to the door, not even bothering to look through the peephole.

Which was the reason she lost her breath when she saw Sam standing there.

"Now?" he asked.

Lizzie swallowed hard, took a step back as Sam stepped into the house and asked, "Now, what?"

"You wouldn't let me talk in the hospital," he said as he closed the door behind him. "You said I was too freaked out, and you were right. I was. I'm perfectly calm now. Can we talk?"

"I suppose so," she said weakly.

They stood in the small entryway, face-to-face but not touching. Lizzie held her breath for a moment, then let it go.

"I've made a lot of mistakes in my life," Sam said.

Great. Now she was a mistake.

"I seem to be capable of fixing everyone else's problems, but I just make a mess of anything resembling a personal life of my own."

Was it confession time? Was he going to apologize? This could be ugly. "You don't have to explain…"

"Let me finish," Sam said. "It wasn't easy to stay away all this time, but I've given you a month to settle in with Jenna. I didn't want to be a distraction while y'all got your lives on track, so I waited. I've kept my distance and left you alone."

Maybe she didn't want to be left alone....

"And now I'm here to tell you what you wouldn't allow me to say when you were in the hospital. I've made a lot of mistakes," he said again. "Loving you isn't one of them."

A smile turned up the corners of her mouth. Butterflies danced in her stomach. "You love me?"

"Didn't I just say so?"

"You did." She wanted to believe him but was afraid. Loving and losing him once had been hard. Another episode would wreck her. "Are you sure you're not still freaked by the whole I-almost-drowned thing? I mean, most of that night is a complete blur, but I do remember more than I'd like, and I know what you saw. I don't want you to confuse relief that I'm not dead with...something else."

He put his strong arms around her, kissing her neck and letting his mouth linger there. "That was a night I'll never forget, but no, I'm not still so out of my mind that I can't think straight."

"That's good." *I guess...*

"I'm better when I'm with you, Lizzie," Sam said in a lowered voice. "I need you. I want to be with you all the time, and yes, I love you."

Her uncertainty melted away, rolling off her, out of her in a gentle wave. "I love you, too," she whispered. "And since you're here, I have my own apologies to make. My own mistakes to confess to." She took a deep breath. "I never gave up on Jenna, never, but I gave up on you. I'm so sorry, Sam, I shouldn't have run away from you, I never should've given up. I won't give up on you again, I swear."

He moved his mouth to hers and kissed her very well. It had been such a long time, Lizzie felt as if the floor was going to fall out from under them, as if the world was spinning too fast. Sam felt it, too, she imagined, as he started to undress her and steer her toward the stairs. She followed his lead smoothly, for a few steps.

"Stop!" she said, planting her feet. "You didn't even ask about Jenna. How do you know she's not upstairs?"

He smiled. "Because Rebecca promised me the girls would be occupied for several hours."

"You set that up?"

He looked pleased with himself. "I did."

"Well, that's not all we have to talk about. I haven't taken a birth control pill since the day I walked out of here and left you sleeping."

"Nice," he said drily. "Remind me of that *now*."

"Better now than two or three minutes from now," she argued.

"Two or three minutes? Do you think so little of me?"

"Well, it's been a while since I had a banana split. I think you'll be lucky to get two minutes out of me." She blushed. When would she learn to think before she opened her mouth? Now he'd think he'd fallen in love with a hopelessly easy woman.

Moving more slowly, Sam continued to undress her. "Do you want kids of your own?"

"Sure, but…"

"But what?" Sam prompted when she faltered.

"But you don't. You made that pretty clear. Besides, you know how I am, and if you don't then you need to learn fast. Yes, I want babies, and if you've decided you want babies, too, that's really great, but you just now told me that you love me, and we're not—" she almost choked on the word "—married, and no matter how much I want you and love you I won't set such a bad example for Jenna…not that she'll know about the sex, but if I were to get pregnant…"

Sam reached into a deep jacket pocket and pulled out a velvet box. "Marry me. I love you, I like you. I don't want to spend another day without you officially and permanently in my life. You've turned me into a forever man, Lizzie." He popped the box open with a flick of his thumb to reveal a tastefully large diamond solitaire in a platinum setting. "Say yes."

Was it possible she could have everything she'd ever wanted? Sam. Jenna. A family…

"Say yes," Sam said again.

"Yes," Lizzie whispered, and with that one word her heart and her world were complete. At the moment that was all she had to say.

* * * * *

The Privileged and the Damned
by Kimberly Lang

Lily needs a fresh start—and, fingers crossed, she's found one. After all, why would any of the hot-shot Marshall dynasty even *think* to look beyond her humble façade? Until she catches the roving eye of infamous heartbreaker Ethan Marshall...

The Big Bad Boss
by Susan Stephens

Heath Stamp, the ultimate bad-boy-done-good, is now rich, arrogant and ready to raze his family estate to the ground. If Bronte tries to stop him he'll happily take her down with him. For Heath Stamp has gone from bad...to irresistible!

Ordinary Girl in a Tiara
by Jessica Hart

Caro Cartwright's had enough of romance—she's after a quiet life. Until an old school friend begs her to stage a gossip-worthy royal diversion! Reluctantly, Caro prepares to masquerade as a European prince's latest squeeze...

Tempted by Trouble
by Liz Fielding

Upon meeting smooth-talking Sean McElroy, Elle's 'playboy' radar flashes red, and she tries to ignore the traitorous flicker of attraction! Yet are these two misfits the perfect match?

On sale from 3rd June 2011
Don't miss out!

Available at WHSmith, Tesco, ASDA, Eason and all good bookshops

www.millsandboon.co.uk

INTRIGUE...

INTRIGUE...

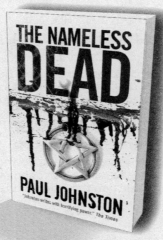

Love and betrayal.
A Faery world gone mad.

Deserted by the Winter prince she thought loved her, half-Summer faery princess, half-human Meghan is prisoner to the Winter faery queen. But the real danger comes from the Iron fey— ironbound faeries only she and her absent prince have seen.

With Meghan's fey powers cut off, she's stuck in Faery with only her wits for help. And trusting a seeming traitor could be deadly.

www.miraink.co.uk

ONE WOMAN'S PRIVATE WAR...

1940, and Vivienne de la Mare waits nervously.
The island trembles to the sound of bombs on the
French mainland. It will be Guernsey next. And
everyone knows that the Nazis are monsters...

Except Captain Lehmann is different...and the
reality of war cannot touch the world they have
built together. Until Vivienne witnesses the casual,
brutal murder of a slave-worker in a Guernsey
prison camp... And her choice to help will
have terrifying consequences.

Available 20th May 2011
www.mirabooks.co.uk

"To say that I met Nicholas Brisbane over my husband's dead body is not entirely accurate. Edward, it should be noted, was still twitching upon the floor..."

London, 1886

For Lady Julia Grey, her husband's sudden death at a dinner party is extremely inconvenient. However, things worsen when inscrutable private investigator Nicholas Brisbane reveals that the death was not due to natural causes.

Drawn away from her comfortable, conventional life, Julia is exposed to threatening notes, secret societies and gypsy curses, not to mention Nicholas's charismatic unpredictability.

www.mirabooks.co.uk

2 FREE BOOKS
AND A SURPRISE GIFT

We would like to take this opportunity to thank you for reading this Mills & Boon® book by offering you the chance to take TWO more specially selected books from the Intrigue series absolutely FREE! We're also making this offer to introduce you to the benefits of the Mills & Boon® Book Club™—

- **FREE home delivery**
- **FREE gifts and competitions**
- **FREE monthly Newsletter**
- **Exclusive Mills & Boon Book Club offers**
- **Books available before they're in the shops**

Accepting these FREE books and gift places you under no obligation to buy, you may cancel at any time, even after receiving your free books. Simply complete your details below and return the entire page to the address below. You don't even need a stamp!

YES Please send me 2 free Intrigue books and a surprise gift. I understand that unless you hear from me, I will receive 5 superb new stories every month, including two 2-in-1 books priced at £5.30 each and a single book priced at £3.30, postage and packing free. I am under no obligation to purchase any books and may cancel my subscription at any time. The free books and gift will be mine to keep in any case.

Ms/Mrs/Miss/Mr _____ Initials _____

_____

Surname _____

Address _____

_____

_____ Postcode _____

E-mail _____

Send this whole page to: Mills & Boon Book Club, Free Book Offer, FREEPOST NAT 10298, Richmond, TW9 1BR

Offer valid in UK only and is not available to current Mills & Boon Book Club subscribers to this series. Overseas and Eire please write for details. We reserve the right to refuse an application and applicants must be aged 18 years or over. Only one application per household. Terms and prices subject to change without notice. Offer expires 31st July 2011. As a result of this application, you may receive offers from Harlequin (UK) and other carefully selected companies. If you would prefer not to share in this opportunity please write to The Data Manager, PO Box 676, Richmond, TW9 1WU.

Mills & Boon® is a registered trademark owned by Harlequin (UK) Limited.
The Mills & Boon® Book Club™ is being used as a trademark.